Love Takes Flight

GAYLE M. IRWIN

Published by Waggin Tales Inspirational Pet Books, 2023.

Love Takes Flight

Waggin' Tales Inspirational Pet Stories

Also by GAYLE M. IRWIN

Pet Rescue Romance
Rescue Road
My Montana Love
Finding Love at Compassion Ranch
Grams' Legacy
Rhiann's Rescue - Pet Rescue Romance Series Prequel
Paws-ing for Love: A Pet Rescue Christmas Story

Standalone
Love Takes Flight

Watch for more at https://gaylemirwinauthor.com/.

This is a work of fiction. Names, characters, business, events and incidents are the products of the author's imagination. Any resemblance to actual persons, living or dead, or actual events is purely coincidental.

FIRST PUBLISHED AS *Rescue My Heart* in the spring 2023 anthology *You Have Made My Heart*. This story updated with new chapters and scenes July 2023.

CHAPTER 1

Eleanor Davis sat on a plaid quilt among the tall tan grasses of a hillside within the Merritt Valley National Wildlife Refuge. The large pond below her vantage point rippled and the marsh cattails dipped their brown heads as a light breeze tickled the landscape. The early May morning brought need for the gray fleece jacket and leather gloves she wore. Mist rose from the wetlands, creating an added chill.

Eleanor shuffled her body and turned the collar up on her jacket before placing binoculars to her face for the third time. She fixed the lens across the pond to observe the pair of sandhill cranes feeding in another swampy area.

The taller male's long beak prodded the wet ground, and the female next to him waded farther into the water. The shadow of a hawk caused the red-headed male crane to raise his long neck toward the sky and produce a rancorous call. Upon spying the soaring hawk, the male jumped from side-to-side, extending his wings as if challenging the bird of prey. The female, smaller in stature, trotted back to her mate, picked up a small stick, and, while tossing it in the air, flapped her three-foot-long gray wings.

"Cool!" she whispered. "You tell him, cranes."

Eleanor then trained her binoculars to the sky and watched a sharp-shinned hawk, its blue-gray feathers distinct in the early morning light, dip and soar as it searched for breakfast.

"Grandad, you'd have loved seeing this," she said in a low voice.

Another crane call, this one closer, reverted Eleanor's attention from the raptor. She used the binoculars to scope out the marsh below her viewing point. The glasses captured the image of a second pair of cranes and also a nearby structure that resembled a beaver's lodge. Eleanor slid off the quilt and haphazardly folded the covering. With binoculars hanging around her neck, she duck-walked toward the structure. However, the cranes seemed to sense her presence. The pair began jumping, lapping their wings, and emitting distress noises. She paused, hoping the birds would not take flight. After they seemed to settle down and return to foraging, Eleanor continued her stealth upon the structure. She leaned against the left side of the camo fabric crafted tent.

"Must be a former duck blind," she muttered.

She took up the binoculars once again, peered around the corner. And focused the lenses on the nearby cranes. She noted the research bands attached to the right legs of the birds.

Eleanor grinned and whispered, "Oh, Grandad – the second pair is back!"

Her excited murmurings must have been louder than she thought for the sandhills began to squawk, and, within a moment, a cacophony chorused from the farther shore.

"I hope you plan to stay put for a while and let the cranes settle down," muttered a male voice from inside the camouflaged tent.

Eleanor squealed and took two steps back. The cranes' rattled bugle calls rose from the marsh, and the two closest to the structure hopped then took a short flight farther away. They landed in a grassy area above the pond.

"I think you've disturbed the birds enough this morning," the graveled voice declared.

STATIONED INSIDE THE bird blind, Nathan Ford hoped his low tone emitted authority.

"Either get in here or move on," he commanded the intruder. "Either way, do it quietly."

Nathan adjusted his video equipment and surveyed the spot where the cranes landed. A moment later, the tent's entrance flapped, and Nathan, dressed in his heavy U.S. Fish and Wildlife coat, took a step back. A moment later, he was face-to-face with a woman bundled in a gray fleece jacket. Her olive eyes stared into his gray ones.

Neither spoke for a moment, and then she said in a hushed tone, "I'm sorry. I didn't realize anyone was here, other than the cranes. I took this for an abandoned duck blind."

"It is," Nathan responded.

He then pointed to the emblem on his down jacket indicating his work with the governmental agency.

"Now it serves as a study sight."

He nodded toward the video camera to his right.

"I'm attempting to find out if this particular pair of cranes will nest on the refuge again this year."

"So, they are the ones who came last spring and summer."

The woman's excited, hopeful voice caught him by surprise.

"Yeah. You know these birds?"

The woman nodded.

"My grandfather and I saw them about this time last year, and off and on, we'd come to the refuge during the summer to see if they stayed. We were happy to learn they did."

Nathan smiled and relaxed his posture.

"It's an exciting time. We haven't had more than one pair stay on the refuge for many years."

He held out his hand.

"Nathan Ford, supervisory biologist."

The woman's eyes widened.

"Nathan? Really?"

"Uh, yeah. I'm pretty sure I know who I am."

"I'm Eleanor Davis, Ellie. I believe you knew my grandfather."

Instantly, Nathan's thoughts traveled back, recalling the times spent at the Davis farm. From his early days as a biologist and purchasing apples and cherries from the elderly couple then a few years later adding vegetables and herbs to his acquisitions to the more recent times as he helped Cal create a small vineyard and construct a larger greenhouse.

"Wow, well, this is a surprise."

The woman's voice brought Nathan back to the present.

"Grandad spoke about you a lot, especially after you helped him with the greenhouse and the vineyard."

The smile she gave him caused the guilt Nathan thought he had buried to resurrect like a prairie flower in spring.

"I, uh, I'm really sorry I ... I wasn't ... I couldn't attend Cal's funeral. I, um, I was ... I was out of town at that time," he stammered.

The smile didn't leave Eleanor's face.

"I understand."

He stared at her. *How could she know?*

"Government meetings, conferences, travel – I get all that. I used to work for the National Park Service. I loved my job, but I sure don't miss all those meetings and travel."

Nathan sighed.

"Yeah, well, there is that."

He turned and picked up the video camera.

"Let's see if I get a bit more of the birds' behavior before I pack up."

Nathan reset the device on the small stand built to hold the camera and zoomed in on the sandhills, now sauntering amid the growing grasses. He took a deep breath. He had been able to keep his struggle from most people. Few knew his real reason for missing the old man's funeral, and he intended to keep it that way.

CHAPTER 2

An hour later, the sun higher in the sky, Eleanor sat beside Nathan on the tailgate of the U.S. Fish and Wildlife Service pickup drinking coffee.

"Thanks for this," she said, raising the mug. "I left my thermos on the kitchen table."

"Do you come out here often to wildlife watch?"

Eleanor, Ellie to her friends and family – well, most of her family anyway – shook her head.

"This is my first full summer at the farm. After Grandad's passing, I still had work with the Park Service. I moved into the house fulltime last month. I hope to spend more time at the refuge this year, but I have so much to get ready for the planting season."

"I'm really sorry about your grandfather – he was a great guy."

Ellie detected sincerity in Nathan's voice. She nodded, and then she gazed upon the refuge, taking in the small flowers pushing through the ground, the aromas of water and bogs, and the singing of meadowlarks welcoming the sunshine.

"Yes, yes, he was. I miss him greatly, both he and Grammy."

"You were close with them?"

Ellie nodded again.

"Very. In many ways, they raised me."

She glanced at Nathan to find him looking at her. Ellie sighed.

Again, looking at the natural scene around them, she answered his unspoken question.

"I've loved the farm since I was a child. I often stayed weekends and then later, as a teen, I'd spend most of my summers with them. Days off from work, when I could get here, I'd come and stay. I helped Grammy with her herb and flower gardens and Grandad with the vegetables. I was back in school during orchard season, but whenever possible, I'd come back on weekends."

"So, where were you stationed while with Park Service?"

Nathan's question was typical for Ellie to answer when people learned of her previous career.

"I spent my last three years at Glacier, which allowed me to visit Grammy and Grandad fairly frequently. Other appointments took me to Yellowstone and Arches, and I spent several winters at Saguaro."

"All great places."

She smiled and nodded.

"I loved each park. Each has its unique beauty."

"What did you do?"

"Fee collection for a few summers then interpretation. I loved the campfire programs in particular."

"Wow, cool! How many years total?"

"Ten."

"And you left to manage the farm?"

Ellie nodded.

"Grandad left it to me."

Each sipped their coffee in silence for a moment.

———— ❧ ————

NATHAN STUDIED ELLIE from the corner of his eye. After his boss told him of Cal's death last year, he had also learned the farm would not be sold, that Cal and Marie's granddaughter inherited the place. The one time he had stopped to offer condolences when he returned to the valley and to his job, no one was home. He found excuses, like work, to avoid stopping in again. Guilt was a heavy load to carry. Now, sitting next to her, he could remove that backpack.

"I stopped at the house once to offer my sympathies and see if I could help in any way. No one was home at the time. Then, the spring work began piling on. I was never so happy to welcome summer seasonals as this year!"

Ellie chuckled, and Nathan found he enjoyed her laugh.

"I understand. It's never easy being a one-person show, especially as the projects arise."

Her eyes met his.

"I appreciate your effort, and I really appreciate your friendship with my grandparents, especially when I couldn't be there."

Their eyes locked for a moment, and Nathan found himself drawn to this woman. Her olive eyes glimmered with a shade of amber. He took in the soft contours of her face and interpreted a sense of strength in her profile. Momentarily, his mind reflected upon the photograph of Ellie displayed on a bureau in the Davis' living room. Wearing a Park Service uniform, the photo showed a woman smiling, reflecting the joy of her job, standing near Delicate Arch in Utah. He also recalled a collection of photos hanging on the kitchen wall, pictures of Ellie at different parks in uniform and in civilian clothes as well as of her at the farm.

"Your grandparents became like my own," Nathan found himself saying. "They certainly were proud of you."

Ellie smiled.

"You saw all the photographs, didn't you?"

He smiled.

"Hard not to. Like I said, they were very proud of you."

She sighed and gazed again at the pond.

"I lost them too soon."

"What about your parents?"

She looked at him.

"If you knew my grandparents as well as you seemed to, you likely know some of that drama."

Nathan nodded slightly.

"Some, yeah. I thought maybe Cal exaggerated."

"Why do you think I got the farm instead of my father?"

Ellie jumped from the tailgate.

"Well, I have animals to tend to and a house to prepare. I'd best get going."

Nathan stepped down and stood beside her.

"What's happening at the house?"

"My cousin is coming to spend the summer with me, helping me at the farm. I pick her up from the Centerville airport in a few days."

"Centerville? Wouldn't Missoula have been just as good or better?"

Her eyes locked onto his again.

"I try to limit my trips to Missoula."

"Ah, parents."

She nodded.

"Dad parent mostly."

She handed him the coffee mug.

"Thanks for the coffee ... and the crane lessons. I, uh, I enjoyed our time this morning."

"Yeah, me, too."

She held out her hand. After another glance at her face, he thrust out his, and they shook hands.

"Listen, if you need help at the farm ...."

She gave him a brief smile.

"My cousin Madison is my helper."

"I know, I understand, but if you need an extra hand, I'd be happy to help. Out of respect for your grandparents."

Really, dude? Lame excuse. Well, it's true!

Ellie's lips curved into a smile which Nathan quietly acknowledged he enjoyed.

"Well, there may be a small construction project or two. I'll let you know. And thanks."

She walked toward the refuge gate where he saw a Subaru Forester parked. He noted the green color and smiled.

Not government issued but definitely a reflection of her previous work and her enjoyment of the outdoors.

Maybe I should have let you introduce us after all, Cal.

Nathan gazed at the sky as the sun took deeper root into the morning.

Or, perhaps, this is the right timing.

CHAPTER 3

Ellie stood in the small wooden corral that enclosed herself and two horses next to the sixty-year-old wood-stained barn. She brushed the black and white paint that had been her grandfather's saddle horse for the past ten years. To the far right, a dark palomino nibbled hay from a trough. The late afternoon sun stood above the western mountains, casting an apricot glow upon the snow that remained on the highest peaks. Eleanor basked in the serenity of her surroundings and the brushings she provided to her favorite horse. Once Grandad's saddle mare, Grace now belonged to her, and she delighted in the camaraderie the two shared amid a shared grief.

"We both miss him, don't we, Grace?"

Ellie's whispered words caused the horse's ears to twitch.

"I'm sure you wished he was doing this instead of me, eh, girl?"

Grace snorted, causing Ellie to chuckle.

"Well, thank you. I'm glad you're accepting me. I'm sure you and Abby over there are glad to be back at the farm with which you're familiar instead of being boarded at Mr. Flanagan's place."

Grace snorted again and shook her head. Ellie laughed.

"Okay, okay. At least the two of you were warm and well-cared for. Mr. Flannagan is a nice guy, a good friend to Grandad, so be thankful he agreed to keep you and Abby for several months while I finished with the Park Service. We'll be getting those mini-donkeys and goats in a few weeks, so you and Abby will have company."

Ellie stopped the grooming to survey the property that now belonged to her. Set in a valley between two mountain ranges, about a half-mile from the foothills of the eastern peaks, the 80-acre parcel served as her source of refuge since childhood. The original homestead house, a two-room log cabin built by her great-grandparents, remained at the back of the property near a wide stream that once served as the source of water. The structure, now a storage facility for equipment, like gardening tools, lawn mower, and snowblower, remained in good shape.

Grandad took great pride in this place, his childhood home.

Ellie's thought created a sense of sadness as an image of her father, who never liked the farm, popped into her head. She shook that cobweb.

"Not going there," she murmured.

Grandad constructed the newer house, the home in which her father grew up. It, too, was made from logs. Two full levels plus a third story with half the space, welcomed family and visitors. The first story, partially dug into the ground, served as food storage when harvest came from the large outdoor garden, the greenhouse behind the residential house, and the orchard, situated to the north and west of the family home. The terraced vineyard occupied the acreage near the homestead house and garden for greater access to irrigation water from the stream.

"I just can't understand why Dad wanted to let this place go?"

Ellie's murmuring brought Grace's head closer, as if listening. Ellie patted the horse's neck.

"This is such a wonderful place. I'm so blessed."

Grace snorted again and bobbed her head, as if agreeing. Ellie chuckled.

"Yes, Gracie, and I have you, too. And Miss Abby."

She glanced toward the other horse. The palomino raised her head at the sound of her name.

"Come here, Abby. I've got some other goodies for you."

The pregnant mare lumbered toward Ellie.

"That's it, girl. Good girl, Abby."

Ellie dug into her coat pocket and pulled out two large carrots.

"I found some in the cellar earlier. One for each of you."

She held out her hands and each horse put the vegetable into their mouth and began to crunch. Ellie smiled and then sighed. She scratched each horse's chin.

"I wonder if you two remember Nathan who came and helped at the farm a time or two?"

The mares seemed to listen to Ellie's murmuring.

"I can't believe I felt such a strong pull when we were together. As many men as I worked around the past ten years, I haven't had that feeling be so strong and so soon. I guess the loneliness has crept up on me, especially since Grandad's passing."

She gazed at the Lincoln Mountains to the west and sighed again.

"Oh, well. When Maddy gets here and summer comes in full throttle, there won't be time to feel alone. And I won't be – Maddy will be here and so will you and the other animals coming our way. No need to wallow or feel lonely, right, girls?"

Both horses nickered, causing Ellie to chuckle once again.

NATHAN DROVE HIS BLUE Ford 150 from the US Fish and Wildlife Service office parking lot. He turned the truck left onto the state highway. His home in Roandale lay fifteen miles north of the community of Paulson, where the agency housed its district office. The thirty-mile daily commute added to the miles he put on his official government truck with the seven miles one way from the office to the refuge or, as was becoming more frequent, the seventy miles one way to the Sweeney Refuge on the eastern side of the Merrick Mountains. He hoped to pass more of those duties onto Jason, the district's newest biologist, hired last year to assist Nathan's sandhill crane study. The younger man had spent the day at Sweeney, setting up wildlife cameras throughout the site in hopes of capturing wolverine activity. A transplant of those large mammals two years ago from Forest Service land outside of Glacier National Park created cause for the study to see how the species fared.

The farther he drove, the more the pull Nathan felt to take a detour. As his vehicle came upon a set of mailboxes on the right side of the road, Nathan glanced at the metal gathering. The painted word DAVIS caused him to again think of the old man from whom he had often purchased apples and vegetables but whose funeral he had not attended. The reason for his absence particularly gripped him. A flash of Ellie's face came to mind, and he slowed the pickup, making the right-hand turn onto the narrow, paved road leading to the Davis farm.

CHAPTER 4

E llie provided more hay for the two horses, keeping them separate in the corral as they ate. She hung the currycomb on a nail on the side of the large red barn. She leaned against a railing and again assessed the property with her eyes.

For the ten thousandth time, Ellie wished her grandparents could enjoy watching the farm flourish with new life. Losing Grandad the previous fall shocked the family and the valley community. The reading of the will brought more shockwaves.

"What do you mean, Eleanor inherits the farm? They were my parents."

Her father's explosive words ricocheted through her heart. Her unwillingness to sell the land, despite her father's incessant insistence for more than a month, created a deeper chasm in the family.

"You really do stupid things, Eleanor. I don't know why you're so headstrong on this idea. My own father struggled to make that farm work; nothing changed from the time I was born until he died."

"A lot of things changed, Dad," she had retorted. "The greenhouse, the vineyard ..."

But Bruce Steele Davis wasn't finished with his word whip.

"We need to sell the property and take the money — land brings in a lot of bucks in western Montana. Selling that farm will make sure all of us are taken care of for the rest of our lives — your mother and me, your brother, and you."

"That's why Grandad left the farm to me and not you."

The two hadn't spoken since that exchange last Thanksgiving.

Clopping horse hooves brought Ellie back to the present. Grace walked over and placed her white velveteen nose upon Ellie's shoulder, tickling her neck. Ellie smiled.

"You always know when I step toward that dark place, don't you, girl?"

She patted Grace's neck and then wrapped her arms around the horse.

"Why have I always had an affinity for and connection with animals more than people?"

Her whispered words remained for the horse's ears only.

"Except Grandad and Grammy. I'm grateful for this amazing gift of land and the new goals and dreams it provides, but I sure do miss them."

Grace's black ears twitched, as if processing her human's words. Ellie began stroking the mare's broad shoulders,

"We're going to do this, Grace. We won't let Grandad and Grammy down."

She took hold of the horse's halter and gazed toward the west. Although the sun remained, providing light and heat, touches of rose and apricot hinted at the upcoming evening and sunset. She heard and then noticed a vehicle traveling toward the farm's driveway. She watched the sapphire blue pickup pull into the driveway.

"Who in the world could that be, Grace?"

Ellie released the horse's halter and walked a few steps toward the far corral rails. She caught her breath as she watched Nathan jump from the driver's seat. He smiled and waved.

NATHAN WALKED TOWARD the corral. He saw the two horses and grinned as he recalled the few times he and Cal had taken the animals down the road to the Spring Creek Trailhead, oftentimes spending two or three hours exploring the Forest Service land behind the Davis farm. He understood why Ellie sought to keep this place – the rich soil, the breath-taking scenery, and the deep serenity were things no one could, or should, put a price tag on.

As he drew closer to Ellie, he called out, "I know I didn't tell you I would stop by, so I apologize for just dropping in."

"No, no that's fine. I'm just surprised to see you."

Nathan stopped at the wooden fence and again gazed at the horses. Ellie walked over and stood next to him.

"Cal really loved these horses," Nathan commented.

"Yes, he did. Grace in particular."

Nathan looked at her.

"Are they adjusting? To his absence, I mean?"

Ellie shrugged.

"I think so, little by little. They stayed at the Flannagan place over the winter. Abby is going to foal in a few months, so I'll be giving Mr. Flanagan the youngster when it's old enough to leave its mother. He's giving me two bum lambs to start my little petting zoo. I'm getting chickens for eggs, so I hope a few of them will be kind enough to tolerate kids."

Nathan studied her.

"Petting zoo? Kids? I sense a story there."

Ellie chuckled.

"Yeah. Variety is the spice of life, they say, so, in addition to the normal fruit, veggies, and herb offerings at the Davis Family Farm, we're going to have naturalist-style programs for families, including a petting zoo."

"Wow! Sounds incredible. And it sounds like you have a lot in the works already."

Ellie nodded.

"I started working on the plan in November. I had hoped at Thanksgiving to help my dad see the opportunity to make this place fun and profitable with the various ways of bringing in money."

"No go, uh?"

Ellie shook her head.

"He said my business plan was a pipe dream and doomed for failure."

"I'm sorry, Ellie."

Nathan couldn't imagine a father not encouraging his child in her dreams, especially someone like Ellie who was not only passionate about her goals, but realistic and intelligent enough to draw up a business plan.

"I've come to expect such things from him. Still, I can't say I wasn't disappointed."

Their eyes met momentarily.

"What brings you by? I'd have thought you'd be headed home from work."

"I am. But I drive by here every evening I'm in the office. I live up the highway in Roandale."

She nodded.

"Nice little community."

"It is. I only wish I had been able to buy some acreage when I relocated to the valley."

"Land's gotten really expensive in western Montana."

"All across the state."

"So, why'd you stop by again?"

Ellie's eyes held Nathan captive. His heart skipped a bit as they looked at one another.

"Well, I wanted to see if you might need help with anything this weekend. The weather is supposed to be sunny and fairly warm for this time of year. I don't have anything going on, so if I can help here at the farm, I'd be happy to."

"Nathan, you don't need to spend your free time working – you have little 'me time' as it is, I know that all too well. You'll be busier than ever in less than a month – enjoy whatever weekends you have left before summer season kicks in."

"I want to help you, just like I helped your grandad. You have a lot of work ahead of you, and because Cal was my friend, I don't mind lending a hand."

She studied him for a moment.

"Well, if you're sure, I could use a bit of help before my cousin arrives."

"Name it – what can I do?"

"I have a list in the house of things I'd like to accomplish before Memorial Day weekend. I'm planning an open house to let people know the Davis Family Farm is still here and that we intend to continue my grandparents' legacy."

"Tell you what – you grab the list, and I'll put the horses in the barn. We can go down to Patton's Pizza, have some dinner, and go over the list, prioritize some things, and you can tell me more about this business plan and the petting zoo."

"I can whip us up something ..."

He held up his hand.

"I dropped in unannounced. Least I can do is get us some pizza."

She smiled, and Nathan felt his heart palpitate once again.

"Okay. Sounds good. Abby goes into the larger stall. I'll be out in a minute."

Ellie scurried toward the farmhouse. Nathan watched her for a moment and then turned his attention to the horses.

"Okay, girls, time to get you settled for the night."

CHAPTER 5

Sitting across the table from Nathan in a booth at Patton's Pizza, Ellie turned over recent events in her mind: acquiring the farm, the feud with her father, developing a business plan with her cousin by phone and internet chats, and the recent encounters with Nathan. The past six months, and the last twenty-four hours, brought dramatic changes to her life.

Now, as she listened to him talk, Ellie found the man captivated her. His easy-going demeanor, his dedication to her grandparents, especially Grandad, and his passion for conservation, intrigued her ... and spoke volumes to her to the type of man he was.

She studied his face while he spoke. Not only did they share the mission of conservation, but his charming smile, square-shaped jaw, and rugged appearance created butterflies in her stomach, a feeling she had not experienced in many years.

"After an interim at the Charlie Russell Wildlife Refuge in central Montana and travelling the state, I got on at Benton Lake where I worked for a couple of years," Nathan said. "When the supervisory opportunity opened up here four years ago, I applied and was hired."

"So, you cover Merritt Valley Refuge, supervising the other biologists and summer help?" Ellie asked.

Nathan nodded.

"And the Sweeney Refuge east of the Merritt Mountains. They're umbrellaed under the same district office."

"That's a lot of land to cover!"

He grinned and nodded.

"Glad we have official vehicles, especially on days I drive east."

A waitress brought their pizza, and Nathan thanked her.

"Refills on your drinks?" the young woman asked.

Nathan looked at Ellie.

"I'm good," she said.

"Me, too. Thanks anyway, though," Nathan remarked to the waitress.

"Let me know if you need anything. Enjoy."

"Thanks again," he responded.

Ellie reached for a slice of the large Italian sausage, mushroom, and black olive pizza. Her fingers touched Nathan's as he, too, reached for a slice.

"Oh! Sorry," Ellie said, and she jerked her hand back as a pulsating charge went up her arm.

"No, my fault. Go ahead," Nathan said.

Ellie tried to smile as she again reached for the pizza.

"Smells delicious!"

"Have you ever been here before?"

She shook her head as she placed the pizza onto a small, white plate in front of her.

"My grandparents weren't pizza people. Grammy was an excellent cook, and she enjoyed making food for people. I was able to take them out to that lovely German restaurant on the lake near Centerville a few times, including their forty-fifth wedding anniversary. We also took a few dinner cruises on the lake, primarily for birthday celebrations or at the end of harvest season. Otherwise, we ate at home or occasionally in Missoula."

As she took a bite of pizza, Nathan asked, "So, why is your dad so set against keeping the farm?"

"Money. Grandad knew the place was at risk if he left it to my dad, so he insured I inherited the farm to protect it."

"Wow."

"Yeah."

Another moment went by as each nibbled their slice of pizza. Then, Nathan prompted, "So tell me about this idea of a petting zoo."

"I'm bringing in some rescue animals, including a dog and two cats, two mini-donkeys and three goats. I'm also getting two bum lambs and some chickens, as I mentioned. I plan to offer farm tours and educate people, especially children, about how to grow things and take care of animals as well as teach them about the landscape and the wildlife in the area."

Nathan looked at her.

"Like an environmental education program."

Ellie nodded.

"Maybe even a summer camp in the future."

Nathan smiled.

"Well, that's your expertise. Doing interpretive programs for the Park Service gives you that added knowledge and experience. I think it's a fantastic idea."

She looked at him and smiled briefly.

"Thanks. I really appreciate that. Only my cousin really supports the idea. Even my mom, who's come to my defense several times, thinks I'm foolish."

UPON IMPULSE AND INSTINCT, Nathan reached his hand across the table and enfolded one of Ellie's,

"I'm really sorry there's this conflict with your dad. Doesn't make life easy."

She didn't draw away.

"No, but it was easier when my grandparents were alive. We were three against his one ... or two if you count my brother."

"He sides with your dad, I take it?"

Ellie nodded.

"I felt bad for Grandad – neither male in the family did much to see the farm succeed."

"Well, at least he had you. And, you have me."

Ellie bit her lower lip and slowly withdrew her hand from Nathan's grasp.

"Nathan, I ..."

He sat back in his seat.

"I'm sorry. That was a bit much."

He looked into her eyes again.

"Look, I know we just met ...."

She chuckled.

"Yeah, uh, this morning."

"I know, I know. Yet, your grandparents spoke of you often. They were so proud of you! And after your grandmother passed, Cal, well, he sang the praises of his beautiful, intelligent, dedicated granddaughter, a woman with passion for nature and sharing that passion with the world. I came to know you through him and all those photos. And then, today, I get to meet this wonderful person he spoke so often about."

He noticed tears glistening in the corners of her gray-green eyes.

"He said all that?"

Nathan nodded and leaned forward again.

"The pride in both their voices as they told me about you was wonderful to hear. I often felt I knew you on some level although we'd never met. And now, we have."

Nathan took a deep breath and continued, "Your grandad was strong; I see that in you, too, Ellie, but no one can do everything alone. I'd like to see you succeed with that farm, and I'm sure you will. Just as Cal let me help him with some things, let me help you. I'd like to stand alongside you and be someone who cheers you on. Like Cal did."

She smiled slightly.

"I can't quite picture you as my grandad."

He grinned.

"Good."

Their eyes locked again for a moment. Ellie looked away first. She toyed with the napkin next to her plate. Nathan decided to break the tension.

"So, show me that list you made while we finish this pizza."

CHAPTER 6

The next morning, Ellie hiked the Spring Creek Trail above the farm. An overlook along the path was her destination, an expansion of boulders from where explorers have a wide view of the valley. Each step brought fragrances of glacier lilies, shooting stars, and fairy slippers, growing amid the greening grasses. Ellie maneuvered around the dainty plants in their yellow, pink, and lavender attire. A chipmunk scurried amid the foliage, bringing a smile to her face. The familiar path and bright spring day warmed her heart.

Ellie arrived at the rock outcropping and chose a large boulder on which to sit. Her eyes scanned the view, the pastures, fields, and homes along the valley floor and the tree-covered Lincoln Mountains to the west. Several clear-cut swaths exposed areas of large log houses, metal roofs gleaming in the mid-spring sun. She looked at the nearby mountain peaks, the bright blue sky embracing them with light and recalled some of the conversation shared last night with Nathan as they finished the pizza and drank a favorite valley brew.

"Your grandfather helped me out when I first arrived," Nathan told her. "I met him at the hardware store – we were both buying tools to fix our houses. When I learned about the farm, I became a customer. No better vegetables around."

"Did you ever try my grammy's herbs? I know she had the tastiest mint, and the teas she made were fantastic!"

Nathan had smiled.

"Basil, rosemary, and thyme were some of my favorites – I must admit, I could make some mean spaghetti sauce with those herbs!"

"Oh, Grammy's recipe for sauce and for chili – the best you've ever had!"

Nathan's grin challenged her.

"I bet my spaghetti sauce could even beat your grammy's!"

They agreed to a sauce cookoff after her cousin's arrival.

"But, she can't be the only judge," Nathan had said. "My friend Jason needs to be in on this, too."

After the teasing, he added, "I fully intend to continue being a customer with the farm. And I'll ask Jason to help out with some of the projects on your list. A few of them are going to require more hands than you and I have."

"I won't turn down another set of hands," Ellie had responded. "I just don't want to keep you from your work or your own home chores. Or your friend."

Nathan reassured her they could manage to help her and keep up with their obligations.

"Besides, I drive past your road twice a day. I'm already in the area often, and Roandale isn't that far from the farm."

Now, gazing at the breath-taking view and absorbing the sights, sounds, and smells of nature in western Montana, Ellie felt gratitude bubble within. Thankful for her grandparents, for the farm, for the lands around her, for the serenity of spring, and for a new friend and encourager, she opened her arms wide and whispered, "You've given me an amazing gift, Grandad. I hope I can make you proud. I want to succeed at this, for you and Grammy. And for myself."

SNAP!

Ellie whipped her head around at the sound. Her eyes traveled from brown hiking boots and chocolate-colored pants upward to the face of a familiar tan-shirted U.S. Fish and Wildlife Service employee.

Nathan grinned.

"Why am I not surprised to see you here?"

AS HE GAZED AND SMILED at Ellie, Nathan took in her serene face. Not for the first time, his heart raced.

Slow down, dude, he scolded himself.

"May I sit?" he asked aloud.

Ellie nodded and moved a bit.

"You startled me."

"Sorry," Nathan said as he sat next to her. "I was coming down the trail and caught my foot on some gravel. I sometimes forget this part of the trail can be steep going down."

"What are you doing up this way? I thought you'd be at the refuge checking on the cranes again."

"Jason, my colleague, is doing that. I'm out scouting for bear activity. You brought bear spray, didn't you?"

She patted the green fanny pack at her waist.

"I don't go hiking without it."

"Good. I saw a lot of sign further up the trail. They're feeding on the new grass and flowers."

"This is as far as I'm going today. I just needed a short hike to get the blood and brain flowing this morning."

Nathan grinned.

"Short hike of nearly a mile incline."

Ellie returned his grin.

"Nearly twenty-five years of walking, working the farm, and hiking, and ten of those years with the Park Service – not difficult to stay in shape."

He quietly agreed with her assessment. He withdrew trail mix from his daypack, made up of almonds, cashews, peanut butter bites, and chocolate chips. He tilted the bag toward Ellie.

"Need a power charge?"

"Thanks – just a smidge though."

He smiled.

"Smidge? That's a Marie word, isn't it?"

Ellie's smile brought a glow to her face, he noticed.

"Yeah. My dad picked it up, too, so I guess it's a family word."

Nathan poured some of the trail mix into Ellie's hand.

"By the way, Jason agreed to help with the construction project at the barn. We'll be at the farm Saturday at nine. Does that work for you?"

The smile remained on her face, and she nodded.

"The coffee will be on. I appreciate both of you. Maddy might be a bit jet-lagged, but I'm sure she'll be ready to join us before eleven."

"Where's she coming in from again?"

"New Mexico. She's been a student at New Mexico State down in Las Cruces."

"Art major, right?"

Ellie smiled wider.

"You were listening."

"Of course. We talked for quite a while, if you remember."

"Yeah, sorry about that. I've been at the farm for more than a month without much company. I'm sorry that I prattled on."

"Don't be," Nathan replied. "I learned how much we have in common, and it's easy to talk with a person with whom you share common interests."

"So true. I still can't get over you worked with the whooping crane project in Wisconsin – I followed that for years!"

Nathan grinned.

"It was a phenomenal program to be part of. I want to go back there some spring and watch the whoopers return."

"That would be amazing. Even going to Florida in the winter after they've migrated would be a wonderful experience."

Jason nodded.

"You said last night you thought you'd have lettuce, spinach, onions, and beets I can buy this weekend?"

"Not quite. I said I'd be able to give you some this weekend. It's the least I can do for your help at the farm."

"And I said I'd be a customer. That means I buy vegetables. And you will be successful, Ellie. I am sure of it."

A blush crept to her cheeks.

"You heard that, uh?"

"Yeah, well, and from what you've told me, I know that's something that weighs on you."

As she gazed at him, Nathan felt resolve well up within him. He kissed her cheek gently, and his mind spoke words he could not yet utter aloud.

And I'm going to be there for you to help you succeed.

CHAPTER 7

That afternoon, Ellie stood inside the Merritt Valley Humane Society lobby. As she signed adoption papers, the woman behind the counter said, "Remember, we know little about any of these dogs. The obvious thing is they had little socialization with people, so each has a level of timidity, and the female you're adopting is one of our most timid."

Ellie looked up and smiled.

"That's why I'm getting the cats as well. I think they'll keep each other company on the occasions I have to be away."

"Well, you chose a fine pair – Cecilia and Victor are siblings, and they adore one another. They're friendly with people and good with other animals."

"And you tested them with the collie, correct?"

The woman nodded her head.

"The cats were curious. Linda didn't know what to think of them, but she didn't lunge or even try to run away."

Ellie whisked her signature upon the final page and handed the paperwork to the animal caretaker.

"I still can't understand how or why a person would have forty collies and Shetland sheepdogs and think they could care for them all. If border patrol hadn't checked that horse trailer ..."

She shook her head.

"Some breeders only see dollar signs," the woman responded. "Border patrol checks all cargo these days; how the person thought they could cross the border with all those animals is beyond me."

"Maybe the people secretly wanted to get caught, knowing in their hearts they were in over their heads."

"Maybe. Whatever the case, each dog is getting a new loving home. Thank you for being one of the adopters."

Ellie smiled.

"My grandparents had two collies when I was a little girl. Grandad always said they made the best farm dogs, and now that I run the farm, and I knew you had obtained the confiscated collies and sheepdogs, I decided I wanted to have another dog at the farm. I'd have taken two if you'd let me."

The woman smiled back.

"We had so many applications for these dogs! Once news hit about them, we were inundated with phone calls and emails. People even showed up at the door, thinking they could just come and get one. Your place and situation seem ideal, and truthfully, working with just one of these dogs is likely best. Once she's used to you and her new home and you've created a bond, bringing in a canine friend for her, one who is confident, will likely be good for her. Meantime, the idea of the two cats as friends for Linda is really excellent."

"Well, as I told you, my cousin is coming to stay the summer, and she loves cats. Since she's been in college, she hasn't had pets of her own, so having Victor and Cecilia will be a delight for her as well as for me and Linda."

Ellie paid the adoption fee for the two cats and the collie. Then, the shelter worker said, "Let's take the cats to your car first, then we'll load Linda. I take it you have everything you need now for the adoptions?"

Ellie nodded.

"In addition to the cat carriers, I picked up food, litter, a dog bed, and some pet toys on my way over. They're all in the hatchback of my car. The cat tree I ordered arrived the other day and is already set up next to the picture window in the living room."

The woman nodded.

"Excellent! Let's get those kitties for you."

Ellie picked up the two carriers from the counter and followed the woman to a room off the lobby.

AT THE WILDLIFE REFUGE, Nathan stood next to the driver's side door of his charcoal-colored government pickup. Binoculars to his eyes, he used the lenses to sweep the wetlands of each pond. At the front of the truck, his colleague, Jason Barrett, used the pickup's hood to balance a spotting scope, as he, too, scanned the area.

"It's exciting to see two pairs of sandhill cranes on the refuge this spring," Jason stated. "You think they'll stay all season?"

"I think if they stay into next week, they'll stay all summer. If we don't see them next week, then we'll know they've moved on."

"Too bad they don't have bands, or at least on one of them. It'd be nice to track them this year."

Nathan nodded.

"At least we know our usual banded pair has returned. This is their fourth year in the valley."

"Think they might run the other pair off if those ones do decide to stay?"

Nathan shook his head.

"There's plenty of nesting and feeding grounds for both pairs. Our regular couple seems to be hanging out where they nested in previous years, so this new pair, provided they stay, has plenty of habitat to make their own home."

"I hope we see them before heading back to the office — and I hope they stay this summer."

Nathan glanced at his friend and grinned.

"More work for you."

"It's not work if you love what you do."

"Amen to that, brother."

They remained quiet as each studied the landscape. Not far away, a western meadowlark warbled. Another returned the call. A male mountain bluebird darted from tall grasses to low-growing shrubs, gathering insects on which to feed. Among the cattails, red-winged blackbirds sang, and overhead the spring sun cast shimmers upon the nearby waterways.

"Beautiful afternoon — a great time to be in the field," Jason commented.

Nathan smiled.

"No place better to be, except maybe in the mountains."

"Fortunately, we can do both."

"Another 'amen.'"

The two men looked at each other and grinned.

"Well, I'm not seeing the new pair of cranes," Jason stated.

"Me either. They might be in another part of the refuge."

"Or they've moved on."

"We'll try in the morning before I have to head over the pass to the Sweeney River Refuge. It was early morning when I saw them before."

Each man gathered equipment and loaded items into the cab of the truck.

"When you met Miss Davis?"

"Yeah, that's right."

Jason climbed into the passenger's seat as Nathan sat behind the steering wheel on the driver's side.

"And tell me again how I'm helping you help this woman?"

"Some repairs are needed on the barn, and she wants to expand the greenhouse. She's already ordered the lumber and plastic sheeting. She thought the sprinkler system in the vineyard may have a few broken spickets – we're going to tackle the repairs first, on the barn and in the vineyard, and then get to work on the expansion."

"That's going to take all summer! What did you sign me up for, Nathan?"

Nathan turned the ignition.

"It's not going to take all summer. Some of Ellie's neighbors, friends with her grandparents, chose the weekend after next to help with the project, so between you, me and six other men, plus Ellie and her cousin, we'll get it done in two days or less."

"A good ol' fashion barn raisin'" Jason quipped.

Nathan grinned.

"In this case, a greenhouse raisin'" he said.

Nathan's cell phone blipped. He checked the text message and smiled as he read Ellie's words.

I got them! Linda, Victor, & Cecilia are settling into the farmhouse. I'm super excited!!

He texted back.

Great news! I'm happy for U.

"What's that smile on your face?"

Jason's question caused Nathan to look at him.

"Smile?"

"Yeah. All dopey-looking."

"Oh, stop!"

"No, man, I mean it. You got a secret love you haven't told me about?"

Nathan put the truck in drive.

"No, just good news from a friend."

"Uh-huh. Sure."

Nathan didn't respond as he began driving along the two-track road leading to the refuge gate.

CHAPTER 8

The next morning, Ellie sat in a green recliner near the living room's large picture window. The cat tree she had ordered and set up provided a viewing stand for her newly-adopted cats. Victor lay in the circular top, lounging as he observed black and white chickadees, red and gold finches, and tiny pine siskins nibbling seeds from an outdoor bird feeder while downy woodpeckers and brown-capped nuthatches feasted on suet enclosed in a black wire cage. Cecilia's tail switched as she, too, watched the little songbirds from her perch on the window ledge.

Linda lay on a dog blanket by the stone hearth, amber eyes darting right and left. Ellie glanced at the dog and murmured, "You're fine, Linda girl. This is home now. You can relax."

Cup of coffee in hand, Ellie turned her gaze to the outdoors. She smiled as flashes of yellow, black and white, red, and gold darted around, out of, and into the feeders.

"This was one of Grammy's favorite things about the farm," she said aloud to the animals. "She loved feeding and watching the birds."

Ellie then looked toward Mount Lincoln, the highest peak in the area, amid the western range bisecting the valley as it traveled south toward Missoula. A wave of sadness crept over her as she noted the numerous houses dotting the foothills and traveling more than half-way up the towering peak, its top still covered in snow.

At least the timberline section still remained wild, providing hideaways for the wildlife and views for valley residents.

A bald eagle's cry reverted Ellie's attention from the mountain range to the sky. The large bird dipped and soared above a nearby field, likely looking for a rabbit or pheasant. She never tired of viewing the area's wildlife or hearing their calls. The eagle dove into the pasture across the road from the Davis farm. The white-headed bird of prey returned to the sky, a small rodent in its claws.

Well, there's breakfast for you, Mr. Eagle.

Ellie looked at her four-footed charges nearby. She noticed Cecilia straining her feline neck toward the left side of the window.

"And that is why, Miss Cecilia, you and Victor will never be let outside. There's plenty more birds of prey out there just waiting for cats to roam."

The grey tortoiseshell looked at Ellie and responded, "Meow!"

Ellie laughed.

"Is that an argument or an agreement?"

Her cell phone rang. Ellie checked the caller ID and smiled upon seeing her cousin's name. She answered.

"Hey there, lovely cousin! About to board a plane?"

"Yep, in about 40 minutes. You all set for some company for three months?"

"Most certainly! You'll have new family members to meet."

"Oh, wow – you did it!"

Ellie's smile deepened.

"Sure did. Two kitties and a gorgeous collie await your arrival."

"Ellie, I'm even more excited to spend the summer with you."

"I know how much you miss having some furry creatures to hang out with. And, what's a farm without a dog and a few cats?"

Hearing Madison's joyful chuckle caused Ellie to smile. Having the animals even just one day filled her with deep joy, too.

"We're going to have a blast this summer," Madison said.

"That we will. We already have a customer for the vegetables and fruit, so when you get here, there's going to be a push for planting. I want to restore Grammy's herb garden, too."

"You still have Grandpa Cal's customer list?"

"Of course. I made sure I had the most updated version at the end of the summer season, and after I was able to have access to his computer upon his passing, I pulled up the fall fruit customer list and updated that on my computer as well. Everything is set for mailing, by email and postcard. I know you haven't had time to draft anything..."

"Oh, bite your tongue, Miss Eleanor Davis! I definitely have a draft. Started it two days ago and just finished it. I'm sending it to you to look over as soon as we hang up."

"Maddy, I can't believe you had any moments to spare, between finals and packing."

"When I get inspired, I get inspired! And after you shared more about your dream of rescue animals and creating Grandpa Cal's Animal Barn, well, a design idea just morphed."

"Now I'm all the more excited!"

"Okay, check your inbox in five minutes. Gotta go! Boarding soon and I want you to see this idea and meditate on it as I wing my way north. See you soon, cousin!"

Madison clicked off, and, with a smile, Ellie followed suit.

Ellie looked at her adopted animals and then gazed upon the outdoor setting of hills, mountains, pastures, and the little birds that still flitted among the feeders.

"Thank you, Grandad, for entrusting me with this special place," she murmured. "Maddy is the perfect partner, and we will do right by your legacy."

NATHAN DROVE HIS PICKUP along the highway, heading to the office for another day of work. He slowed the truck as he approached the turnoff at the group of mailboxes on the left side of the road. The black letters which spelled DAVIS stood out. He punched the left turn signal and headed the truck down the paved road toward the farm.

As the pickup ambled along, Nathan double-checked the two coffee containers in the console, ensuring the lids remained secure. After calling Ellie earlier with an offer to bring caramel mocha in exchange for meeting the new farm pets and then receiving her permission, his heart constricted as the truck came closer to the Davis driveway. He drummed his fingers on the steering wheel and hummed a tune from a decade ago. Then, he chuckled to himself.

"Face it, dude," Nathan said aloud. "She intrigues you, and yes, you're attracted to her."

He turned left from the road and into the Davis driveway while trying to steady his rapidly beating heart. Nearly three years had passed since he experienced these feelings. As he placed the truck in park, he hoped for a better outcome this time.

CHAPTER 9

E llie sat on her grandmother's green wicker rocking chair on the front porch of the farmhouse, sipping the coffee Nathan had brought ten minutes earlier. He sat nearby, appearing comfortable on Grandad's over-sized chair. She studied his face from the corner of her eye, his black hair and complementary beard and mustache trimmed neatly. The morning breeze lifted his dark locks, adding to the rugged features of his tan face.

"Thanks for the coffee – it's a great warm up," Ellie commented. "I could have made some here."

Nathan smiled.

"I don't leave home without it. Besides, I couldn't expect you to make the coffee after I practically invited myself here."

"Well, you did say you wanted to meet the animals and get some vegetables to go with your lunch today."

He nodded. "I did say that, yes. That collie is a beauty! And your cats – I'm surprised how friendly they are."

Ellie smiled.

"My cousin is going to gush all over those kitties. I think they're helping Linda settle in easier, too. Do you have pets, Nathan?"

He shook his head.

"Too busy in the field."

Ellie nodded.

"I get that."

Each took a sip of coffee. Afterward, Nathan asked, "I hope you don't mind me getting some vegetables today. I know it's early in the season, but with the greenhouse ..."

She smiled as she looked at him.

"Yes, that greenhouse has plenty of produce coming on, including some lettuce, sprouts, and tomatoes."

Nathan's dark eyes widened.

"You must have started those pretty early."

"I started several crops early. I wanted to get a head-start on the season."

Ellie sipped her coffee and then asked, "When did you decide being a biologist was the pathway for you?"

She noticed Nathan gazed upon the mountains in front of the property.

"I got into Eagle Scouts as a teen and though I lived in the city, we did a lot of camping at state parks and I learned a great deal about the outdoors. By the time college rolled around, I decided to attend Western Illinois University and got my bachelor's degree in biology. I specialized in zoology and minored in botany. I worked for the Illinois Department of Natural Resources for a few years then moved to Wisconsin and was with the DNR there for several years while pursuing my master's at Madison in environmental conservation."

"When and why did you move to Montana?"

After a sip of coffee, Nathan responded, "After getting my master's, I joined the U.S. Fish and Wildlife Service and worked at Horicon Marsh. I had worked on the state portion of the marsh when I first arrived in Wisconsin. A year on the federal side of the marsh, I transferred to Necedah National Wildlife Refuge."

Eleanor raised her eyebrows.

"Isn't that where whooping cranes were introduced and then later taught to fly to Florida?"

Nathan stared at her.

"Yeah. You know that project?"

She nodded.

"I followed it for a few years when it first got started. I thought the project was very exciting!"

Nathan smiled and said, "I was there for the second year of the program and was able to monitor the whoopers' activities."

"Wow! That's awesome!"

Ellie didn't hide her admiration for Nathan as she smiled at him.

"You all did amazing work there," she said. "Cranes are thriving more now with the work you and others have done and are doing."

"That's one of the great aspects about being a biologist – helping conserve and preserve species."

He took a sip of coffee and then asked, "What about you? Tell me more about your time with the National Park Service."

"Like you, I started with the state. While in high school and college, I worked with Montana Fish, Wildlife and Parks, working at some of the parks during summers. I went to the university in Missoula and received my bachelor's degree in parks, tourism and recreation with a minor in environmental policy. Later, after a few more years working fulltime for FWP, I attended the University of Idaho and received a master's degree in natural resource management with a specialty in environmental education."

"Doesn't the University of Montana offer something like that?"

"They were just getting started at the time – Idaho had their program in place, especially for environmental ed, and it was well-recognized."

He nodded.

"Good choice then, I guess."

Each took another sip of coffee. Afterward, Nathan asked, "Your dad's a businessman, right? Do you get your enjoyment of the outdoors from your mother?"

Ellie nearly choked on her coffee as she laughed a bit.

"Heavens no! The enjoyment of nature and being outside comes from my grandparents. For some reason, it skipped my other family members. Mom would prefer to live in Spokane or even Seattle, but Dad stayed in Missoula for his job and for his parents, I guess. He's an only child, and he's been with his company nearly forty years. He'll be retiring, or should I say, he can retire, in a few years, but he loves money too much to leave the company. They'll probably have to force him out to get him to leave."

"I take it your parents weren't too supportive of your choice of major and employment?"

Ellie shook her head.

"Much to my father's chagrin, I always wanted to work for the Forest Service or the Park Service."

Nathan grinned.

"He preferred you work for my agency?"

She shook her head.

"He preferred I went into business, like him and my brother. I wanted to work in outdoor recreation, particularly environmental ed and interpretation. Truthfully, I didn't think many opportunities existed with the Fish and Wildlife Service for that or I would have considered your agency. I didn't want to work inside a visitor's center all the time, though."

"Can't blame you – I much prefer outdoor work, too."

As she looked at him and noticed his biceps and rock-hard chest, she murmured, "Obviously."

She caught his eye and quickly looked away.

NATHAN DETECTED A HINT of admiration in her soft voice, just as he had a few moments ago while they talked about the whooping crane project. He hid a smile. He enjoyed the thought that their career paths were similar and that she knew about the Wisconsin program.

"You're good for my ego," he said.

She looked at him and her sea-green eyes and auburn hair captivated him once again.

"Where have you been all my life, Eleanor Davis?"

Did you really just say that, dude?

Nathan quickly stood up.

"I need to get to work. How about some of those tomatoes and lettuce you were telling me about?"

CHAPTER 10

D riving into the parking lot at the airport the next afternoon, Ellie scanned for an open spot. She glanced at Linda, the tri-colored collie, securely buckled into the backseat of the Forester. The dog had been quiet during the twenty-minute ride from the farm to the Centerville airport. Upon finding an empty space, Ellie maneuvered the Subaru into the slot. As she put the vehicle in park, she again felt gratitude for her cousin, who paid extra to fly into the smaller airport instead of landing in Missoula. One complication with her parents averted by encouraging Maddy to choose Centerville as her destination.

"Closer for me to pick you up anyway," Ellie had told her cousin.

She even offered to pay the additional plane fare.

"Hey, you're letting me live with you rent-free for three months. I can pay the additional fee to fly into a smaller airport," Maddy had said.

"But I'm also making you work those three months."

"You're also getting me out of New Mexico when I need it."

They agreed to a special dinner the evening of Maddy's arrival, a quiet spot along the lake to eat, drink, and catch up. Then, Ellie adopted the animals, so the dinner plans changed. She promised her cousin an evening out within the first week.

"After a day of sweat and toil, we'll go somewhere fun," she told Maddy.

"Deal!"

Now, as she prepared to exit the Subaru, Ellie looked at Linda again and ruffed the dog's soft fur.

"You hang out here, sweetie. I'll be back with Maddy in a short while."

Wafts of gray clouds hung in the sky, offering proof of the weather forecast for rain that night. She stepped out of the car and set the Forester's locking system. Then Ellie began walking toward the terminal. A brisk breeze caused her to pull the hood of her jacket over her head.

She knew the minestrone soup in the InstaPot would taste good this evening, along with the loaf of wheat bread she had purchased from the local Amish market. She had also bought cheese, honey, mushrooms, sweet peppers, and chicken. Fresh lettuce leaves, cherry tomatoes, and sprouts from the Davis Family Farm greenhouse awaited her and Maddy for a salad to complement the soup. Her stomach growled thinking about the upcoming evening meal and flip-flopped in anticipation of spending the upcoming months with her cousin.

Ellie entered the terminal. Centerville's airport was small, but busy, especially in the summer with the tourist traffic, people who visited Glacier National Park, the surrounding forest lands, and the large, nearby lake. Outdoor enthusiasts and shoppers alike took in the landscape and the small towns along the highways that connected the majestic national park to the bustling town of Missoula. Stores of all types, including western wear, gift shops, art galleries, natural body and home products, ice cream parlors, and bars dotted the streets of communities along the lake and the state roadway running north and south. Ranches also made up the landscape, including resorts catering to tourists who wanted to ride horses and sleep in cabins. Signs of various types in the terminal welcomed travelers and advertised services, including hiking, mountain climbing, mountain biking, eco-tours, and boating and fishing excursions.

Ellie stopped at a brochure rack and removed some literature about art galleries, lake cruises, and the two summer theater houses, things she knew her cousin would likely enjoy.

Two planes stationed at two different gates lingered for the loading and unloading of passengers. Ellie scoured the arrival board. Upon seeing Maddy's flight number, she turned to her right and walked to the proper waiting area. The first people to exit the plane began milling around the luggage carousel. Another small group arrived, and among the passengers, Ellie spotted her cousin. With a large smile, she held up her hand and waved. Maddy saw her and, with enthusiasm, waved back. Ellie held herself in place, but inside, she felt like popcorn in the microwave. About eight months had gone by since she had spent time with Madison, and that time, the passing of her grandfather, had been shrouded in sorrow. This time, excitement and anticipation, rooted in their reunion.

The carousel began turning as the distance between Ellie and Maddy shrank. Within moments, they were hugging, laughing and crying.

"Goodness, girl! It's been way too long," Maddy said.

"Hasn't it though? I'm so glad to see you!"

"I bet I'm more glad. Let me look at you."

They stepped back from one another and sized each other up.

"Still as gorgeous and fit as ever," Maddy commented.

"Oh, no! But look at you! Goodness, how do you find time to hit the gym while pursuing a master's degree?"

"I just followed your advice – get out every day and walk at least thirty minutes. Sometimes that's the only thing I could do. Then, other days, especially after Stewart and I broke up, I'd run three miles a day just to release the energy."

"Yeah, heartbreak does that to a person."

"Running or eating a box of Twinkies – some days I did both."

Ellie chuckled and hugged Maddy again and said, "But you're here now. All of that's behind you, and this summer there will be no guy trouble. It's a time of healing and creating."

She stepped out of the embrace to find Maddy smiling.

"I'll drink to that. Oh, I guess that comes later. Let me get my bags."

Ellie grinned.

"I have a surprise for you in the car."

Maddy's eyebrows raised.

"An easel?"

"No, I'd never dare buy one of those. You get to pick that out yourself. But a subject for at least one summer painting."

This time, Maddy's brown eyes widened.

"The collie?"

Ellie nodded, smile still on her face.

"Oh, I can't wait to meet her! And, we have to stop by an art store on our way to the farm. Just flying here and getting a glimpse of the scenery has spurred my creative juices, and I'm sure the farm will further stimulate my senses."

"I have no doubt, dear cousin, no doubt at all!"

ON THE REFUGE, NATHAN and Jason sat in the government pickup. Each man held a pair of binoculars to his face.

"I think I see them," Jason said.

Nathan looked at him, and Jason pointed northwest. Nathan glassed the area and spotted two sandhill cranes several hundred yards away, near the edge of a marsh.

"I think it's the unbanded pair," Jason whispered. "I don't see anything on any of the legs."

Nathan focused the lenses upon the birds and studied each one closely. No bands, no wing monitors.

"Uh. Maybe they are staying. If so, this will be the first year in nearly a decade that the refuge has hosted more than one pair during the summer."

"That'll be great news, won't it?"

Nathan glanced at Jason. His colleague's smile was contagious. Nathan grinned back.

"Most certainly!"

He pulled a small notebook from his backpack and set it on the console between him and Jason. The younger biologist continued studying the lanky birds. As he began to jot down notes, Jason's next statement startled him.

"Nathan, I think I see a nest."

Nathan looked at Jason and then out upon the prairie. He tried to look in the direction his colleague seemed to be viewing.

"Where?"

"Slightly to the right of the birds."

Nathan picked up his binoculars again. Upon locating the cranes, he moved his observations slowly to the right. Soon, he spotted a large, round mound of sticks and grasses a few feet from the large birds.

"By golly, I think you're right."

He gazed at the scene a few minutes more.

"She'll be laying eggs soon, I'd speculate."

The men remained quiet for a few moments, each observing the adult birds and the oval-shaped creation that might become home for one or two sandhill crane eggs.

"So, do you think we'll have a second pair of sandhills calling the refuge home this year?" Jason asked.

"I'd bet my job on it."

"Yes!"

Jason's outburst caused Nathan to look at him, and he grinned.

"Definitely exciting."

A thought crossed his mind. He removed his cell phone from the holster attached to his belt. He texted Ellie.

Second pair of cranes established a nest. More birds at the refuge this year!

"What are you doing?" Jason asked.

"Telling a friend the good news."

"Supervisor Stevens? You could just wait til we get back to the office."

Nathan smiled.

"No. Someone else who enjoys sandhill cranes as much as we do."

"Oh. Her."

Nathan shook his head as he returned his phone to its case. "You really like this woman, don't you?"

Jason's question caused Nathan to look at him and then out the truck window.

"We have a lot in common."

"A good thing in a relationship."

Nathan shrugged, trying to act nonchalantly.

"I suppose. There's no relationship, just a friendship."

"But you'd like it to be more than that."

Nathan ignored Jason's comment. His friend picked up one of the tomatoes Nathan had brought from the farm.

"Fine-looking vegetables she gave you. Thanks for sharing, by the way."

Nathan grinned.

"Lots more coming on in the greenhouse for next month. Ellie has her grandfather's growing skill. I hope the grapes survived – Cal began making wine last year and that would add another element to his granddaughter making a go of the place."

"And that's important to you?"

Nathan looked at Jason.

"Yeah, it is."

"You have it bad for this woman, my friend."

He bit into the tomato as Nathan started the truck's ignition and buckled his seatbelt. He again chose to ignore Jason's comment.

"Time to head back. We have some paperwork to fill out before quitting time."

"Great tomato," Nathan stated as the truck ambled down the dirt road. "Whenever you have more to share, I'll take some."

"Become a customer and get your own. Support a local business, you can afford it."

"You could just share with your colleague, but no. Shows me you definitely have it bad for this Ellie woman."

CHAPTER 11

Ellie and Maddy sat in the living room, sipping red wine from the bottle of cabernet Ellie had set out earlier. Dinner finished, the two women sat in quiet companionship, having spent more than 90 minutes at the table enjoying a meal and sharing vision for their summer together.

"I need to say again, Maddy – that's an incredible design you've created for the new logo. I'm excited to see it finished!"

Her cousin smiled.

"Glad you like it. Now that I've seen some of the animals as well as the landscape, I can finish the artwork and we can get postcards printed and emails ready. There's only a few weeks to plan this event."

"True, but I want you to take time for yourself as much as possible and stand at that easel you purchased today. Use those canvases. This is not just a summer of working on the farm, but of finding yourself again and the beautiful paintings you create."

Ellie took a sip of wine and then added, "I'm glad you found what you wanted here in the valley. Saves us a trip to the big city."

Maddy chuckled.

"Big city. Let's see, if I remember correctly, Albuquerque is about ten times bigger than Missoula."

"Yeah, but how long has it been since you lived in Albuquerque? Nearly a decade?"

Maddy shrugged.

"But I still visit occasionally. Anyway, I'm glad, too. I'd rather be here than driving to Missoula, at least for the time being. I imagine you don't desire to spend much time there these days."

"You've got that right. This is my happy place. Missoula and my parents' home – not so much."

She raised her wine glass and tilted it toward Maddy.

"Here's to us and all we will accomplish these next three months!"

Maddy smiled and raised her glass as well.

"I'll drink to that!"

As they chimed their wine goblets, the two women chuckled. Just then, Cecilia the cat, jumped on Maddy's lap, startling the woman and nearly spilling the wine.

"Oh, girl!"

Madison's scramble to upright the crystalline stemware and prevent Cecilia from toppling off her legs caused Ellie to laugh again.

"She's a sneaky one!"

Maddy stroked Cecilia's back.

"I didn't expect her to become so comfortable around me this quickly."

"They're both the friendly sort. Neither are very shy," Ellie said.

"They are both just gorgeous! I can't believe they were in an animal shelter."

"It's heartbreaking, Maddy. There must have been sixty cats at the humane society in our little valley! And about thirty dogs in addition to the collies they rescued. I understand it's happening all around the country. After COVID restrictions lapsed, in less than a year so many shelters became overcrowded and rescues could hardly keep up."

Maddy shook her head.

"Same down in New Mexico. Like you said, it's happened all over."

She took a sip of wine.

"Well, thank you for rescuing these guys. When I go back to New Mexico, I'll adopt again. Now that the jerk is out of my life and I can get my act back together, once I settle somewhere I won't be without a pet again."

Each woman sipped her wine.

"This is so delicious!" Madison said. "This really came from Grandad's first crop of grapes?"

Ellie smiled and nodded and then replied, "He was full of surprises."

"And you said there are two cases in the basement?"

Ellie nodded again.

"I plan to use them when we have the open house."

"Well, it will knock people's socks off! So, tell me more about this biologist you met and the sandhill cranes."

"His name is Nathan Ford, and he helped Grandad put in the vineyard."

Maddy's dark eyes widened.

"No kidding?"

Ellie smiled.

"No kidding. And he helped with the greenhouse, which, by the way, is producing lettuce, tomatoes, sprouts, and green onions already. Nathan's already purchased some of the produce, and he's telling his work colleagues we're opening for fulltime business soon."

"Wow! This is so exciting, Ellie! We're going to be busy women this summer! So, tell me more about this Nathan – he seems like good advertising for the farm."

The smile remained on Ellie's face as she responded, "Yes, he is. He enjoyed being around Grammy and Grandad – I think he looked to them to fill the hole of missing family. He's originally from the Midwest, and he began helping the grandparents, especially Grandad, here at the farm."

"And you never met him when you were here with them?"

Ellie shook her head and sipped from her wine glass again before replying.

"No. I guess he was here on days I wasn't."

"And he didn't come to Grandad's funeral?"

She shook her head again.

"Away on business as I understand. He's the supervisory biologist for the wildlife refuge just up the highway a little way. I took you there a few times."

Maddy nodded.

"Nathan sent me a text earlier today saying there are more cranes on the refuge, which is exciting because it's been years since more than one pair nested there. If another pair claims territory this summer, that will be exciting."

Maddy raised her wine glass.

"Another toast. To an exciting, fun, productive, and healing summer – for both of us."

Ellie smiled and again tapped her wine glass to Maddy's.

"I'll drink to that as well!"

NATHAN STOOD ON THE back deck of his home in Roandale. The small community along the shore of Merritt Lake glimmered with patio lights from residential homes as well as from bars and restaurants along the shore. Most of the time Nathan enjoyed the sights, but with the upcoming onslaught of tourists, the increased volume of noise as well as light imposed on the tranquility he usually enjoyed.

"One day, I'm going to own a piece of land outside of town," he told himself for the millionth time since choosing this house nearly four years ago.

A group of pelicans caught his eye, and he watched the chubby, white birds glide closer to the lake. He counted about a dozen, and he continued watching them as they circled once above the nearby boat dock and then seemed to choose a safe place to land on the lake. One reason Nathan had selected this house was because of the wildlife that came to the area despite the houses and businesses and the ability for him to enjoy nature as well as small town amenities. Still, he longed for a piece of land like he had enjoyed in Wisconsin prior to moving to Montana. At least his job offered the benefit of being outdoors and away from town ninety percent of the time.

Tempted to call Ellie, Nathan remembered her cousin was to arrive today. He felt the need to talk with someone, so he punched the speed dial for his father. After three rings, Andrew Ford answered.

"Hey, Dad. How's your evening going?"

Nathan waited for a response and then said, "Yeah, good. Did you get the photos of the sandhill cranes I sent earlier?"

Another pause.

"Yeah, isn't it great? If they all stay the summer, we could have the best year for cranes at the refuge in more than twenty years."

He listened and then laughed.

"Yeah. Not often when you can say having three pair of sandhills is record-breaking for two decades, but, with all the development that's happened over here during the past nearly quarter-century, well, you know how that goes – it happened in the East, then the Midwest, and along the Pacific Coast. When habitat's destroyed, what does the wildlife do?"

Nathan listened to what his dad said for about five minutes.

"Well, I sure do hope you and Mom get out here this year. It's been too long since we went fishing together. And I ... I ... um, I hope to introduce you to someone I met the other day."

Another pause, then Nathan chuckled.

"Yeah, yeah, Dad, she's a woman. Remember me telling you about Cal Davis, the older gentleman with the farm and orchard?"

A slight pause, then Nathan continued, "Yeah, well, I finally met his granddaughter – she now owns the farm, and she has this amazing vision to add other elements besides the fruits and vegetables. You got a few minutes? I'd like to tell you what she told me – it's pretty incredible."

Nathan sat on one of the Adirondack chairs on the deck.

"Great. I think you're going to be impressed. I know I was."

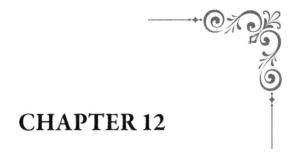

CHAPTER 12

The next morning, Ellie padded down the farmhouse hallway in her black, ballerina-style slippers, her cotton pajamas enveloping her in warmth from the chill of the spring sunrise. The scent of brewed coffee welcomed her into the kitchen, as did the appearance of the recently-adopted cats. Each rubbed against one of her legs.

"Well, good morning, friends! Maddy got up much sooner than I expected."

She leaned down and stroked the chin of both cats.

"Did my cousin already feed you and you're mooching me for more?"

Victor presented a loud purr and raised his head for more attention. Cecilia continued rubbing her body against Ellie's leg. She chuckled.

"You are moochers, both for food and for attention."

She glanced into the living room and saw Linda lying on the oversized dog bed.

"And how's my favorite pup this morning?"

The collie remained stoic.

"We'll go for a walk soon, girl," Ellie told the dog.

Ellie then walked to the refrigerator and drew out a can of tuna-flavored cat food. She set it on the counter and removed the covering.

"I believe Maddy did feed you, my kitty friends. There's less in here than there was last night."

She removed two small bowls from an overhead cupboard.

"Just a smidge more, as Grammy would say."

She took a teaspoon from a nearby drawer and placed a small scoop of the cat food into each dish. She then placed both bowels on the kitchen floor and removed a coffee mug from the cupboard. After filling the mug first with the hot liquid and then with a serving of almond creamer from the refrigerator, Ellie walked into the living room. She leaned down and patted Linda's head.

"Where's Madison, my friend?"

The collie gazed into Ellie's eyes. The sorrow and uncertainty she had noticed on adoption day continued to reflect in the luxury-coated dog's amber eyes.

"You're safe here, Linda. No need to be anxious. This is your home now, and no one will hurt or neglect you anymore."

Ellie tousled Linda's brown and black neck ruff. The silkiness delighted her. Although she knew the history of this dog and her canine companions, she also knew about the gentle, loving treatment they received after the rescue. The many months spent at the shelter and the numerous volunteers who assisted the staff in socializing and caring for the abused animals brought vibrancy to the dogs' coats, teeth, and other physical qualities. Ellie only hoped that would translate to Linda's eyes and her demeanor. Obviously, that would take more time.

"You're going to be fine, sweet girl. Maddy and I are going to spoil you rotten!"

As she straightened up, Ellie glanced out the picture window. As she sipped her coffee, she watched her cousin, standing at the easel, a canvas on the stand and her paint palette and brush in-hand. Ellie smiled. Her eyes took in the scene that brought Maddy outdoors with her artist's supplies. Wispy clouds lingered near the mountain peaks as the morning sun rained rays of light, like lasers, upon the jagged peaks. Primrose, lavender, amber, and cream filled the sky from east to west, enveloping the greening valley. Grace and Abby stood in the corral, facing the rising sun, as if bathing in the beams and enthralled by the new day.

"I can't wait to see how she captures this day," Ellie murmured.

A ring from her cell phone startled her, breaking the trance of the May morning. She checked the caller ID, and, with a small smile, answered.

"Good morning, Mother. Heading off to work?"

She listened a moment and then responded, "Yes, Maddy made it in just fine. We enjoyed a lovely dinner, talked a lot, and now she's already outside painting."

Ellie smiled as she made the statement. She remained silent as her mother spoke and then said, "No, we haven't made any concrete plans for the entire summer yet – Maddy just arrived. But, we've added some animals to the farm. I was able to adopt one of those collies from the court case a few months back, and I also adopted two cats, siblings, hoping not only to please Maddy, but to help the dog adjust better. So far, so good."

She listened for a few moments again and then stated, "Well, let's give Maddy a bit more time to settle in before you or dad come visit. We're going to be busy replanting some of the gardens and settling animals in during the next week or so. Let's look at getting together in a few weeks."

She sipped her coffee and again listened to her mother's words. She frowned and then responded, "I know two weeks seems like awhile, but truly, Mom, we need to get some work done around the place, and I'm sure Maddy wants to get some painting done, like she's doing this morning. Let's give her a bit of time."

Another moment of listening and then Ellie said, "Look, Mom, I know you have to leave for work, and I need to get breakfast for Maddy and me. I'll call you this weekend and we can talk more about this, okay? Bye!"

She clicked off and muttered, "Oh, bother – just what I need, Mom's meddling."

She returned her gaze out the window and noticed Grace moved from the edge of the corral to the feeding trough.

"Breakfast time for everybody," she murmured.

NATHAN DROVE THE U.S. Fish and Wildlife Service pickup along the Sweeney River. The rocky canyon outside of the small-town Brewster kept the early morning sunrise from reaching the river. Whenever he traveled to the other refuge he managed northeast of Missoula, he had to leave early in the morning or travel the night before. Yet, he relished this time of the day for the decreased traffic and increase in wildlife viewing opportunities.

As a curve in the highway approached, Nathan slowed the truck's speed. He glanced at the rocky cliffs to his left and scanned for the hopeful sight of bighorn sheep. He grinned and decreased the vehicle's speed again as a pair of ewes, each with a lamb-of-the-year, came into view. The mothers cropped the grass near the roadway while their youngsters nursed. Nathan edged the truck into the passing lane, giving the sheep a wide berth and, therefore, less disturbance. A roadside pullout came into view, and Nathan turned on the truck's signal light and eased the pickup into the parking area near the river. After stopping the vehicle and setting the gear in park, he unbuckled his seatbelt and reached for the thermos in the side pocket of the driver's side door. He then poured himself a mug of fresh coffee.

Nathan surveyed the river, flush with run-off from the mountains surrounding the canyon. Rolls of water traveled downstream, feeding into the Clark's Fork in the town of Missoula thirty miles away. Various species of ducks, including mallards and pintails, rode the waves while three pairs of Canada geese bobbed along the shoreline.

Nathan picked up the receiver of the radio unit in the truck and called into the federal office back in Merritt Valley.

"Dispatch, this is Ford reporting in. I'm currently in Brewster Canyon, about fifteen minutes out from Sweeney. I'll be there all day preparing for the summer seasonals to arrive. I'll be back on the Merritt side tomorrow."

A female voice responded back, "10-4, Nathan. Enjoy your day."

He grinned and clicked the mic again and replied, "Already am. Bighorn sheep with young in the canyon."

The woman's voice came back and said, "A wonderful way to begin a day!"

"10-4 on that!"

Nathan re-set the radio mic and returned his gaze to the river.

"Dad would enjoy fishing out here," he murmured. "I wonder if Ellie fishes?"

As he shook his head at himself, movement amid the shrubbery at the river's edge caught his attention. A young male moose wandered through the bushes and stood at the waterway. The six-foot-tall bull raised his long nose as if sniffing the air, then looked right and then left, like a child seeking to cross a street. The gangly creature then stepped into the river and began to swim.

Grin on his face, Nathan said aloud, "Now I know Ellie would love to see this!"

He whipped out his phone, pressed the camera key, and zoomed in. Nathan snapped pictures as the animal with a small rack of palmate antlers, found his stride and coasted toward the opposite shore.

Nathan watched as the moose climbed up a small hill and shook the water from his body. The bull began to feed on willows. Nathan took a few more photos. He then texted some of the pictures to Ellie with a note.

Headed to Sweeney Refuge for the day. Saw this guy and had to share a few photos. All the more reason to enjoy the outdoors!

Afterward Nathan continued to observe the moose and finish his coffee. A blip from his phone let him know he had received a text. He read Ellie's response.

Lucky you! Been awhile since I've been over to that side. Might be a nice outing sometime this summer.

Nathan chuckled.

"Might be indeed," he murmured.

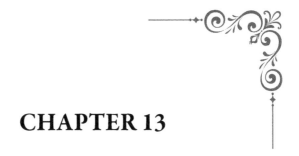

CHAPTER 13

Later that morning, Ellie and Maddy worked side-by-side in the newly-established herb garden. Each took a row to weed by hand, pulling up sprigs of grass and vine weed that attempted to weave among the young rosemary, thyme, basil, and oregano plants that Ellie and placed in the ground last week.

"This is going to be a wonderful garden, Ellie," Madison stated as she wrestled with a stubborn section of vine weed.

"I'm looking forward to the farmer's market starting in a few weeks. The plants in the greenhouse will be ready to sell, and these should be good to go in late June or early July," she told her cousin.

"As long as the rains come like they should."

"I also have more irrigation water this year, thanks to the land exchange that happened last year."

"But don't you want that for the orchard and the vineyard?"

Ellie nodded.

"Primarily, yes. But, if needed, we can use some on the vegetable, flower, and herb gardens."

"That moose your friend Nathan saw earlier today would have been neat to see," Madison commented.

Ellie smiled and then replied, "Wouldn't it? We don't see them around this area as often as we used to."

"I imagine habitat destruction accounts for that."

Ellie nodded.

"And some disease wiped out a bunch about five years ago, I remember Grandad saying."

They continued working in silence for a few minutes.

"Too bad Grandad wasn't here to see us re-establish Grammy's herb garden."

Madison's comment caused Ellie to pause. She gazed at the farm, her eyes sweeping across the pasture where Abby and Grace grazed to the large farmhouse where her father was raised and then farther where the vineyard was planted and the greenhouse stood. Ellie sighed.

"Yeah. They would have been proud of us."

She looked at her cousin.

"I'm so glad you decided to come out here. Not only do I appreciate your help, but I'm glad for your company."

Maddy returned Ellie's gaze.

"This is just what I need right now – a good friend who's like a sister, a quiet space, hard work, and majestic scenery. And rescue animals to love and be loved by."

"The break-up with Stewart was difficult, wasn't it?"

Maddy nodded.

"About like you and Grant, I guess."

Maddy sighed.

"When you spend nearly two years with the same person and you think the relationship is headed one direction and it goes another, and you're not expecting that … yeah, it hit me pretty hard."

"Well, this is a great place to heal. I should know. After having the baby and then still trying to make things work with Grant and that not happening, I spent many months here, working for one of the state parks, yes, but just being here with Grammy and Grandad. The collies were still here then. They gave me great comfort, as did Grace, Grandad's horse."

"I'm looking forward to having the other animals you're adopting. I think those mini-donkeys and Pygmy goats you told me about will be great fun!"

Ellie smiled.

"They will certainly be a draw for the petting zoo! I'm also getting chickens from a neighbor who needs to decrease the number of birds she has ..."

"Ah, fresh eggs for cooking and baking!"

"Another neighbor has two bum lambs we'll also be getting."

Maddy frowned.

"Aren't lambs born in early spring?"

"Late winter around here. These are a specialty breed, and they were born late. Their sibling didn't survive, and mama nearly died, so these two have been bottle-fed for the past month."

"Oh, I think I'm going to love bottle-duty!"

"I might fight you over that job!"

She and Maddy laughed. As they returned to pulling weeds, Maddy spoke softly.

"I'm happy to be here, grateful in fact, and I'm glad to share the next few months with you."

Ellie looked at her cousin and replied, "I'm really glad you're here, too."

CHAPTER 14

The next morning, Ellie stood in the corral brushing Abby. The mare's swollen belly spoke to the birth expected in the next few weeks. Ellie placed her hand on the horse's side.

"Not much longer, sweet Abby. Mr. Ferguson plans to be here to help you, help us actually. I just know you're going to have a beautiful baby," she whispered to the golden mare.

She looked over at Madison, who stood in the vineyard with her paint supplies, and she smiled. Her cousin's creativity unleashed at the farm, and she looked forward to taking Maddy to the Merritt Valley Refuge in a few hours. They had made plans to lunch there and for Maddy to paint the birds they were likely to encounter. Both expressed hope in seeing a sandhill crane or two. Perhaps they would even run into Nathan. Ellie's heart did a flip thinking about that possibility.

As she continued brushing Abby, Ellie chuckled to herself. Just a few days of knowing him and she already felt like a teen crushing on the popular football player. Not only was Nathan physically handsome, but his knowledge and appreciation of nature and its inhabitants matched her own. She thought about their phone conversation last night as he drove from Missoula to his office after the day at Sweeney River Refuge. She thrilled at the thought of seeing female bighorn sheep and their young and developed even greater excitement of his description of the small elk herd he had witnessed and the two pair of trumpeter swans he had discovered on one of the ponds while walking the refuge grounds.

"I really need to get over there again sometime," Ellie had said.

"Let me know when you want to go," he had responded. "We should bring your cousin, too."

"We?"

"Well, I can be your special tour guide, for you and Madison. The wildflowers are just starting to bloom, and I imagine in about two weeks it will be a painter's canvas, so to speak."

"I think ... I think we'd like that," she had said.

The unique call of a sandhill crane caused Ellie to return to the present and switch her gaze from Abby toward the sky. She took a deep breath and exclaimed, "Sandhill!"

Ellie dropped the horse brush and dashed from the corral. She ran toward her cousin and called out, "Maddy, look! A sandhill crane!"

The younger woman turned from her canvas and easel. She skewed her neck and looked heavenward.

"Oh, wow! I thought I recognized that noise but it's been a while since I've heard it."

"I wonder if that's one Nathan told me he saw the other day, one of the new ones."

Ellie, now standing near Madison, kept her gaze on the bird. She watched it glide lower, toward the stream near the back of the property.

"I think it's landing by the creek."

"Probably looking for bugs and worms, maybe getting a drink," Maddy surmised.

"We should keep an eye out, see if it stays, or brings a mate. There hasn't been a sandhill crane on this land since I was a kid."

"I know you love all this nature stuff. Next winter you'll have to come visit me and see the thousands of cranes and other birds that winter at Bosque del Apache Wildlife Refuge. You would love it!"

"I did visit, remember? The second winter I worked at Saguaro."

"Oh yeah. We went and spent a whole day there during President's Day weekend."

"Yeah. I almost didn't get the time off because it was a holiday. But since we hadn't seen each other the winter before, my supervisor asked another seasonal to cover that time."

"Well, next time you come down, maybe you'll bring your new friend with you?"

Maddy wiggled her eyebrows. Ellie looked at her with a furrowed brow.

"New friend?"

"Wildlife guy? Refuge dude? The one who called last night?"

"Oh, Madison, will you stop? I just met the guy!"

"Well, love knows no amount of time, and you have spent time with him the last several days. You like the guy, I can tell."

"He was good to Grandad, and I'm grateful for that."

"I have a feeling you're not just grateful. I look forward to meeting him."

"We made a pact, remember? No guys. This is a summer for us and the farm."

"For me, yes. You? I'm not so sure. You're settled. This is your home. And if he's settled here in the area, who's to say you two aren't right for each other?"

Ellie shook her head.

"Madison ...."

At that moment, her cell phone blipped, indicating a text message. She pulled the phone from the breast pocket of her fleece jacket and read Nathan's words.

Found another pair of sandhill cranes! One coming ur way. Tracking it. Be at ur place soon.

Ellie smiled and looked toward the west. No new crane calls.

"Hey! What's the grin on your face about?"

Ellie looked at Madison, and Maddy raised her eyebrows.

"Wildlife guy!"

Ellie tried not to blush.

"It's about the cranes. Nathan just texted that he and his colleague, Jason, discovered more sandhills at the refuge and that a pair might be heading this way – or at least one of the pair. They're tracking the birds. So, maybe that one we just saw is one from the new pair they discovered."

"Well, cool! Might be neat to have cranes at the farm again."

Ellie looked east of the house, toward the stream that flowed from the mountain behind the farm and watered the property. Heavy brush remained in that section.

"Grandad left that wooded and brushy area natural for wildlife," Ellie explained to Maddy. "With the stream water, a lot of plants grow there. Deer, elk, all sorts of birds, and even the occasional bear feed, get water, and find shelter in that area. I wonder if the crane landed back in there?"

"Well, some biologists are likely to know," Madison commented.

Ellie looked at her cousin and nodded.

"They may want to go back in there."

Madison placed her hands on her hips, cocked her head, and stated, "So, if they're tracking the birds and the bird or birds are here, or coming here, that means Nathan and Jason are coming here, too, right?"

Ellie silently studied her cousin's face for a moment. She looked at her hands, covered in dirt, then at her clothing, stained with dirt and grass.

"Oh, dear. A change of clothing's in order!"

Maddy smiled.

"My thoughts exactly!"

Ellie's phone alerted her to another text.

BTW, if u have more veggies, I'm buying. So is my co-worker, Jason.

Ellie smiled and looked at Maddy.

"Nathan wants to buy some vegetables, and so does his friend."

"Yes, a change of clothes *is* in order!"

The two women dashed toward the house.

AS NATHAN CLIMBED INTO the driver's side of the government-issued pickup, he looked Jason, who was placing a spotting scope into a safe cubby on the passenger's side of the truck.

"I told Ellie we'd be buying some vegetables if she has more ready to sell. That greenhouse I helped her grandfather build is showing lots of life already, like that tomato you ate yesterday. I noticed lettuce, cucumbers, sprouts, and radishes when I was there the other morning. The Davis Family Farm is the best place for vegetables in the summer and fruit in the fall."

"Oh, yeah, there's an orchard, isn't there? I remember when you got produce from her grandfather."

"Cal was a great guy."

Nathan started the truck's engine.

"I'll see what she has when we get there," he said. "Could be part of my dinner tonight."

"Why don't you take her out to dinner?"

"Her cousin just arrived. I'm sure they have stuff already planned."

He put the truck in drive and began to pull out of the parking spot he had made earlier.

"I told you about Continental Divide playing at the Shoreliner tomorrow night, didn't I?" Nathan asked.

"Oh, yeah. I almost forgot. Thanks for the reminder."

"Maybe your 'friend' and her cousin would be interested."

Nathan glanced at Jason.

"Maybe so."

CHAPTER 15

Ten minutes later, Nathan turned the Fish and Wildlife Service truck off the highway and down the half-mile-long county road toward the Davis farm. He tried to quell the pounding in his chest. Excitement stemmed from the discovery of more sandhill cranes in an area where the species had been absent for nearly two decades. Now the possibility of three nesting pairs grew more plausible, and one of those might take up summer residence on land owned by a woman he admired ... and truthfully, was quickly falling for.

"Hey, you okay, buddy?"

Nathan glanced at Jason.

"Yeah. Fine. Just thinking about these birds now returning to the valley. Pretty exciting stuff!"

"And could you also be excited because one of those birds is leading us to a place where someone special lives?"

"Well, maybe, yeah."

Jason chuckled.

"Maybe? Dude, I think you got it bad for this girl!"

"Yeah, I admire her. I respect her. And we have things in common. Is that so bad?"

"Nope. I just want to hear you say you're falling for her."

"Okay, all right. So, what if I am?"

"I think it's great! You haven't been with anybody since ... Ashley, right?"

"No, I haven't. Purposefully. I don't need another disaster."

"So, you think this woman ...."

"Ellie."

"Yeah, Ellie. You think getting involved with Ellie could lead to disaster?"

Nathan looked at him.

"We never know, do we?"

Jason shook his head.

"Nope, sure don't. How long have your parents been married?"

"Nearly forty years."

"Mine have been together almost thirty. Not all relationships end in a disastrous way. In fact, many don't end at all. Look at the glass half-full, buddy."

"I'd like to, but there's my ... problem last year."

"That's behind you, right?"

"Yeah."

"So, it's the past. Leave it there. Everybody makes mistakes and faces challenges. We both know that. Life is life, and the past is the past. Ashley, your addiction, your recovery. Today is today and the future is the future. Live in the here and now. You like this girl, this Ellie? Then, spend time with her."

Nathan looked at him for a few seconds before returning his eyes to the road. About to make the left turn into the farm's driveway, he asked, "How come you're younger than me but smarter than me?"

Jason snorted and then said, "I'm not smarter. I'm just looking from the outside in."

Nathan parked the truck as a woman he didn't know stepped onto the porch.

"Is that Ellie? If so, man, I'm going to give you some competition."

Jason's words caused Nathan to look at him.

"Competition? What are you talking about?"

His friend looked at him.

"You just said you're taken with this Ellie woman, and now, seeing her, I can understand why. I may give you a run for your money!"

"That's not Ellie. I don't know who that woman is. Maybe it's the cousin she told me about."

Jason flashed a grin at him.

"Even better news."

He jumped from the passenger seat and looked at the blonde woman. He grinned at her and then walked toward her. Nathan disembarked from the truck and heard Jason say, "I'm Jason Williams, friend of Nathan's, the guy standing by the truck. We work for the U.S. Fish and Wildlife Service."

The woman smiled.

"So, I see from your uniform. I'm Madison Harris, Ellie's cousin. We've been expecting you. She's in the greenhouse, gathering some vegetables for you guys. So, I understand you're here about a big bird."

Jason grinned as the two shook hands.

"Yes, that's one reason we're here."

Nathan looked toward the large structure he helped Cal construct. He saw Ellie emerge, carrying two medium-sized bags. One brimmed at the top with lettuce while the other appeared to contain spinach. The sweet smile she gave him caused his heart to race.

Jason's right – I've got it bad. Good thing Jason is taken with Ellie's cousin.

For a moment, he thought of Cal.

Why couldn't I have met your granddaughter a few years ago? Before Ashley, before the accident. Before the opioids.

ELLIE WALKED BESIDE Nathan as they sauntered toward the corrals. They had left Jason and Maddy on the front porch talking.

"My friend seems enamored with your cousin," Nathan said in a casual tone.

"Everyone is," Ellie responded. "And why not? She's smart, she's beautiful, she's talented."

They reached the corral and stood watching Grace and Abby as the two horses soaked up the late afternoon sun.

"Interesting. Those are the same words I'd use to describe you."

Ellie looked at Nathan. He kept his gaze on the horses.

"Why, Nathan Ford, are you flirting with me?"

She gave a slight smile as he turned his head toward her. His gray eyes looked into her olive-colored ones.

"Ellie Davis, are you flirting with me?"

A moment of silence passed, but in that moment Ellie experienced an intensity she had not felt in many years. His chiseled face and square chin, the two-day scruffy stubble of hair outlining his features, the dark brown hair cropped around his ears and cheeks yet peeking out from under his ballcap like mischievous urchins tempted Ellie to reach out a hand and brush the protruding curls. Her hand traveled down the left side of his face. Their eyes remained locked as if a magnetic force held them.

Nathan captured Ellie's hand as it trailed down his cheek. Still looking at her, he gently kissed her palm. A jolt, like lightening, zapped her, and as his head leaned down, she closed her eyes. His lips upon hers tasted like a delicacy appetizer she had not eaten in years.

A blip from her cell phone startled Ellie and she pulled away. She checked her phone and found a text message from Maddy:

Jason says the crane is walking on the hillside above the house.

Thought u might want to come & see.

Ellie looked at Nathan. He had stepped away from her, and he cradled his forehead in his right hand.

"Um, sorry about that," Ellie said in a low voice. I'm not ... I'm not usually like that. I apologize."

With one long stride, Nathan stood in front of her.

"I never gave that one thought."

He placed gentle hands on her upper arms.

"We haven't known each other long, but I feel drawn to you like I've never experienced before. I'm thinking ... you feel ... the same way?"

His hesitancy, his question, brought a small smile to her face.

"I do. But, Nathan, I have so much that needs to be done, so much riding on this summer's success at the farm. I can't fail. I can't really be distracted. And you ... you distract me."

"I'm going to be helping you, I told you I would. We'll get to know one another more as we spend time together. I mentioned earlier if that sandhill crane continues returning to the farm, or close to it, I'll need to monitor it. And I'll need your help doing that, keeping some records and notes for me. Are you still willing to do that?"

"Of course! This is important work. You are welcome anytime you need to study the bird ... or birds."

"The work is important. And having your help, and your permission to come out a few times a week to monitor the crane's comings and goings, feeding and other behavior, would be very appreciated."

Ellie took a deep breath and then nodded. She exhaled and whispered, "Well, I guess the work can start now. Maddy said the bird is moving and it's somewhat close to the house."

Nathan smiled.

"Well, I guess it's lesson time on crane observation."

She took a few steps. His hand on her arm stopped her. She looked at him.

"Um, before we do that ...I was wondering ... I wanted to ask if tomorrow, after we work on those projects from your list, would you be interested in going out for dinner and dancing? There's a great Montana band playing tomorrow night at the Shoreliner Saloon. Would you and Maddy like to join Jason and me?"

"Who's playing?"

"Continental Divide."

Ellie grinned.

"I love them! It's been a few years since I've seen them, and I think Maddy would enjoy them, too. Sure. What time?"

"How about seven? I could pick you and Maddy up."

"We should probably just meet you there. Maddy wouldn't take it too well thinking this might be a double-date. She recently experienced a bad break-up, and well, part of the reason she's here is to heal and re-discover herself again."

Nathan nodded.

"Understand. Been there."

"Many of us have."

He looked into her eyes.

"May I ask – how long for you?"

"Almost seven years."

Nathan's eyes widened.

"That is a while."

She shrugged.

"I dated here and there afterward, but I really focused on my career. And my grandparents. I take it your bad break-up wasn't that long ago?"

"Nearly three years. Closer to two-and-a-half, I guess."

"And you're over her?

Nathan smiled and responded, "Completely. I was fairly new to the area and didn't know any better."

He took her hand and looked into her eyes.

"Now that I've met you, I know what's been missing in my life."

He kissed the top of her forehead and smiled.

"Now, let's go see that crane your cousin mentioned."

CHAPTER 16

Ninety minutes later, Nathan sat at his desk in the U.S. Fish and Wildlife Service office. As his fingers tapped the keyboard of his desktop computer, he heard two colleagues talking in a nearby cubicle.

"It breaks my heart to have to leave her behind, but if I don't take this new offer, it may be years before the next opportunity comes around, It's getting harder to move from seasonal work into a fulltime career with all the budget cuts."

"I'd take her, but with my wife's job as a teacher, she'll be going back to work in the fall when the kids return to school."

"Could you maybe foster her for a few weeks until a permanent home can be found? River is great with kids, as you know."

"Let me talk to my wife. It's a possibility."

"Thanks, Michael. That would be a temporary solution anyway."

As the woman walked past Nathan's desk, he looked up and asked, "What's going on, Angie?"

Twenty-seven-year-old Angela Whittaker stopped and looked at him.

"I've been offered a job in Grand Junction, Colorado as range specialist. It's a permanent position with very good pay, and I want to take the job. But I can't find housing that allows large dogs, so I'm trying to re-home River."

"Your parents can't take her?"

The younger woman shook her head.

"Dad's just been given an overseas assignment. They leave in a month."

"I'm really sorry. Glad about the job, that's great, but sorry about you having to be in the situation of giving up your dog. You've had her how long?"

"Four years, and she was already nearly three when I adopted her."

"That's rough."

"I've rarely had trouble finding housing for the two of us, and when there was a problem, Mom and Dad kept her. This time that's not going to work."

Angie's green eyes searched Nathan's face.

"How about you, Nathan? Would you consider taking River?"

He shook his head.

"I'm rarely home – wouldn't be an ideal situation for your amazing dog."

He smiled and added, "But I might know someone."

AT THE RANCH HOUSE, Ellie and Maddy prepared dinner in the kitchen.

"So, you're going to do some bird watching," Maddy commented as she stirred pasta in a large pot of water on the stove.

"I already bird watch. Remember I pointed out the little nuthatch and pair of goldfinches at the feeder a bit ago?"

"I meant the cranes, silly. You get to play biologist."

"Whenever the real biologist isn't able to be here."

"How do you feel seeing Nathan so often? I mean, I know it's his job, to observe and report sightings and behavior, but it's one thing to do that at the refuge and another to be here on your private land."

"It's for the good of science."

Maddy laughed.

"Okay, well, that's a good one – first time I've heard that as an excuse."

Ellie looked at her cousin.

"Excuse for what?"

Maddy returned Ellie's stare.

"Oh, come on, Ellie. I'm not blind, nor am I immune to the crackling electricity between people. You and Nathan have sparks flying between you whether in conversation or not."

"You're being silly!"

Ellie returned to chopping the sweet peppers and mushrooms at the kitchen island.

"You were flushed when the two of you came back from the corral. And he acted nervous. Did he kiss you?"

Ellie sighed and then said, knife mid-air, "I actually kissed him. Or at least I think I did. Maybe it was mutual. All I know is, it was like magnets coming together."

"See! Sparks! I told you!"

Ellie stared across the living room and out the picture window. She took in the mountain view and the greening fields, the white-tailed deer, the robin singing in the large elm tree in the front yard, and the cottontail rabbit nibbling on new grass growing near the tree.

"Do I really need a complication like a relationship in my life right now? No. But, darn, if I'm not attracted to him!"

"So, you could fall for him?"

Ellie looked at Maddy, who seemed to be intently studying her.

"What do you think? I may already have."

She sighed again.

"I've got to be careful there."

Maddy placed a hand on Ellie's shoulder.

"You have a right to be happy."

"I am happy. Oh, I miss my grandparents, yes, and I loved my work with the Park Service, but, even with Grammy and Grandad gone, I feel peace and joy here. Truthfully, after moving around for nearly five years and putting up with a lot of bureaucracy, I was, and am, grateful I got the fulltime position at Glacier and could be here more, especially after Grammy died. I helped Grandad as much as I could having that fulltime job that was still two-plus hours away, but I couldn't be here as often as I would have liked."

"Just think – you and Nathan were both here helping your grandfather but never met during those years. Kind of interesting how that happened."

Ellie's cell phone rang. She checked the caller ID and then showed the screen to Maddy.

"Speaking of ...."

Ellie answered.

"Hey, Nathan – what's up?"

She listened.

"A dog? Needing a new home?"

Ellie glanced at Maddy and then said, "Well, maybe. It's a bit too soon, perhaps, for Linda to meet a new dog."

She listened again.

"Yeah, okay, I'll think about it. You can give me more details tomorrow when you and Jason are here. Maddy and I appreciate your help with the irrigation system for the vineyard and enlarging some of the stalls in the barn. Abby is going to need that extra room in about a month when the foal comes."

She paused again as Nathan spoke.

"Yes, nine o'clock is great. The coffee will be ready and there may be a few cinnamon rolls left."

She smiled and let him talk a bit more.

"Well, great. Yes, I will think about the dog, and I look forward to learning more about her. Maddy and I will see you and Jason tomorrow. And I hope you enjoy the salad fixings I gave you today."

She listened to his goodbye and responded in kind. Then, she hung up.

"What's this about a dog?" Madison asked.

"A colleague of Nathan and Jason's needs to re-home her chocolate lab due to a career move. Nathan wondered if we might take the dog as a companion for Linda and a favor to the co-worker."

"Labs are great dogs!"

"Yes, but is this the right thing for Linda? She's only been here a few days."

"Well, maybe a meet and greet."

"Oh, most certainly! If I decide it's not too soon."

"So, cinnamon rolls, uh? For us or for Nathan?"

Ellie smiled.

"Both. Now, let's get this sauce ready to go and prepare to enjoy our dinner! But save some – Nathan and I have a bet on who makes the best spaghetti sauce, him or Grammy, and since this is Grammy's recipe ...."

Maddy grinned and raised her eyebrows.

"Oh, I get it – just another excuse to see the bird biologist."

Ellie shook her head and tried to hide her smile.

CHAPTER 17

After work that evening, Nathan walked into the Super D Food Mart in Roandale. He greeted a few people on his stroll toward the deli, and as he waited in line, two people back from the counter, a gentle tap to his shoulder caused him to look toward his left. The face of thirty-year-old Ashley Landon came into view.

She smiled.

"Hey there, handsome. Been awhile since I've seen you around."

"Hey, Ashley. Yeah, work's been keeping me busy this spring."

"What about the winter? I thought maybe you decided to become a snowbird. I don't think I've run into you since, oh, what? Last August maybe?"

"Yeah, well, um, I, uh, I had kind of a ... a family emergency. Had things to deal with so yeah, I was gone for a few months."

She frowned.

"Oh, my! Sounds serious. Your mom? Your dad? Not your sweet sister! Oh, my, is Stephanie ...?"

"She's fine, fine. I don't see much of her since she lives in Tennessee, but yeah, she's good."

"Tennessee, uh? What's she doing?"

"Working for a record company and doing her own music."

Ashley smiled again.

"Oh, wow – that's wonderful!"

Nathan noticed he could move forward, closer to the counter, so he took a big step. Ashley accompanied him.

"So, what's new with you?"

Her question gave him pause again. He decided to keep the talk about work.

"We have some additional sandhill cranes at the refuge. We might be banding some birds in the coming weeks."

"Oh. Well, good, good."

"Yeah, it would be great if they all stay this summer."

"So, I suppose you'll be out in the field a lot?"

He nodded.

"Yep, most likely."

A moment of silence passed between them.

"I guess that's why we didn't work out," Ashely said in a quiet voice. "You're always working, I'm always working."

"Yeah, well, the real estate market's hopping around here, I understand."

She nodded.

"I almost had old man Davis' property, you know the one down the road toward your refuge? He had the vegetables and the orchard? I think you helped him with a greenhouse and vineyard one year."

Nathan's heart nearly stopped. He remained quiet, which Ashely used to her advantage.

"That would have raked in millions, I'm sure. At the end of the road, near Forest Service land, with those buildings and gardens! The house was old, but whether a purchaser tore it down and started over or remodeled the heck out of it, that place was worth something. The old man's son wanted to sell, but I learned he didn't inherit the place – the geezer left it to his granddaughter."

Nathan bristled.

"That 'old man,' as you called him, had a name – Cal Davis..."

Her eyes lit up, and she grinned.

"Yeah, that was it! Anyway, I lost a lucrative deal because the buggar gave it to his granddaughter, and she's not willing to sell."

"No, no she's not."

Ashley stared at him.

"You've met her? Did you try to buy the place from her?"

"Ashely, I think ..."

"Hey, there, Nathan. What can I get for you?"

The deli server caught his attention.

"Look, Ashley, I need to get my order and run out of here. Lots to do."

"Yeah, cranes. I got it. Well, take care, Nathan."

She lowered her voice.

"Anytime you want to get together, don't hesitate to call me. I'm always available for you. We had some great times."

After a wink and quick smile, she walked away.

Nathan stepped up to the counter.

"How's it going, Pete?"

"Better if Ashley Landon flirted with me like that. What'll it be?"

I wish she would have chosen you instead of me. Of all people to run into.

Instead of voicing his thoughts, Nathan said, "I'll take the chicken dinner special with pasta salad."

―― ⁓⟡⟋ ――

IN THE CORRAL, ELLIE brushed Grace. The sturdy black and white paint mare stood, a spirit of calm surrounding her. Ellie stroked the horse's back then pulled the brush across her shoulders, and, a few minutes later, down her legs. The animal's eyes fluttered. With each stroke, Ellie also felt tension leave her neck and shoulders.

"I love how you and the other animals de-stress me, Grace," Ellie whispered. "I also love how this place centers me."

She stopped brushing the mare to survey the valley view. Twilight took root, painting the sky with pastel shades of pink, blue, and yellow. The orange sun began dipping toward the horizon, and choruses of Canada geese sang as they flew from nearby fields toward the river that cut through Merritt Valley. The squawking of a sandhill crane captured Ellie's attention, and she gazed at the sky. The long-legged bird with its six-foot wingspan flew over and course-corrected northwest toward the refuge.

"Heading back for the night, are you?"

Ellie's question was directed at the bird. The noise emanating from the crane caught Grace's attention as well, and the mare looked up.

"Seems like we're going to have at least one new neighbor this summer, Grace," Ellie commented, watching the majestic bird wing its way from the farm.

"I just wish Grandad could be here to take in all that's happening with these amazing birds. He would have been so happy to see them return to the refuge and to the farm."

Ellie's phone rang. She checked the caller ID and smiled to see her mother's name appear. She answered.

"Hi, Mom. How are you?"

She listened to Julie Davis' response. The smile remained on Ellie's face.

"I'm glad for you. Congratulations, you deserve that promotion."

Ellie leaned upon Grace's back as her mother continued the conversation. Then, she replied, "Yes, Maddy is here, safe and sound. Tomorrow we begin some of the hard work, with irrigation repairs in the vineyard and creating space in the barn for the new animals, the donkeys and goats I've adopted. They arrive next week."

Another moment of listening.

"Yes, you are most welcome to come on Sunday. We have a small work crew helping tomorrow so Saturday's not a good day, but Sunday should be fine. Most shops that closed for the early spring are starting to re-open. We need to get Madison some art supplies anyway, so yes, come see us! We can make a day of it, the three of us, before we're inundated with work and programs."

She listened again and then chuckled slightly.

"I can't get over the fact Dad and Eric are going on a fishing trip. I mean, I know it's a company retreat, but the last time I remember them fishing was when I was ten or so and Eric was about seven. He and Grandad wanted to go fishing on the lake. Remember, we all went: Dad and you, Grandad and Grammy, Eric and me. We had that big rental boat, remember? Man, did we catch fish!"

Ellie smiled at the memory then sobered, recalling fun times like that were rare.

"So, I'll tell Maddy you'll be here around ten on Sunday. You're welcome to stay the night with us, too."

She listened to her mother and then responded, "Yeah, I understand. Work waits for no one. I'm looking forward to seeing you, Mom. Til then – love you!"

She hung up the phone and laid her head across Grace's back.

"I feel really bad for my mother, Grace. My dad's been a real ogre the last few years, especially so since Grandad's death. Mom tries to keep the peace, and I'm grateful she reaches out now and then. That's the one awful thing about this inheritance – Dad and I can't be near one another."

The mare nickered and leaned her head on Ellie's neck and shoulder. She embraced the horse.

"I love you, too, girl," Ellie whispered.

CHAPTER 18

Saturday morning arrived with bright spring sunlight kissing the valley floor. Ellie stood in the kitchen waiting for the coffee to brew. She heard feet padding down the hall and watched her cousin enter the cheery, yellow kitchen.

Ellie smiled and said, "Morning, Maddy. How'd you sleep?"

Her younger cousin stretched her arms toward the ceiling.

"Excellent! I forgot how wonderfully quiet it is here."

"I'm making coffee. Would you like a cup?"

"Of course! You know I live on caffeine each morning."

"Easy to do as a master's degree student. Have a seat on the front porch – it's a beautiful morning – and I'll be out in a minute."

"Sounds lovely. By the way, those cinnamon rolls smell delicious! You might want to hide them from me – may not be any left for Nathan and Jason!"

Ellie chuckled as Maddy walked from the kitchen. She heard her cousin's footsteps and her voice as she called for Linda. The collie followed her through the living room and out the front door.

Ellie reached into the cabinet above the coffee pot and removed two mugs from the first shelf. She poured coffee from the carafe into each cup and then walked to the refrigerator, pulled out a bottle of almond milk caramel creamer, and returned to the countertop. As she placed a dab of creamer into each cup of coffee, she briefly studied the mugs. Each depicted a scene from the area. One displayed the surrounding mountains and the other highlighted the valley and the major waterway that bisected the area – the Lincoln River. Etched at the top of each mug were the words DAVIS FAMILY FARM. Ellie caressed the letters and sighed. The custom-made cups were a fiftieth anniversary gift to her grandparents from her father. A sweet gesture, Ellie reflected, but still not the lavish gift she thought he would bestow upon his parents for such a feat of commitment.

What will he give mom if they make it to number fifty? A blender?

She shook her head and returned the creamer to the refrigerator. After picking up the two filled coffee cups, she left the kitchen, and the negative memories that sought to overwhelm her. After opening the screen door, Ellie walked onto the porch. Madison sat on Grammy's green wicker rocker, leash handle in her hand keeping Linda close. Dog and woman appeared to be taking in the view and enjoying the pleasant spring morning temperature.

"So peaceful here," Maddy commented in a low voice as she accepted the steaming river mug from Ellie.

Linda looked at Ellie, her long muzzle extended for a scratch. Ellie obliged and then sat near Maddy in Grandad's green, straight-back wicker chair.

"Just wait another month — the highway will be filled with tourists going to and coming from Glacier National Park as well as campers and people who love to fish. Summer is a busy time around the valley."

"As a former park ranger, I'm sure you're used to tons of tourists."

Ellie nodded.

"Don't get me wrong — visitors ensured I and hundreds of others have, in my case, had, work, but honestly, I look forward to an entire summer on eighty acres that belong to our family."

"Technically, your family, not mine."

"Well, your mother and my mother are sisters."

"Yes, but Cal and Marie were your dad's parents."

"True, but Grandad and Grammy considered you part of their family. You were as much a granddaughter to them in their hearts as me."

"They were good people."

The two sat in silence for a moment, sipping their coffee, absorbing the scenery, and remembering the elderly couple that loved them.

After a brief silence, Maddy asked, "So what time are the guys getting here?"

"Nine o'clock."

Ellie checked her phone and then stood.

"Just enough time to eat some breakfast, shower, and prepare for a day of work."

Maddy stood, too, and coaxed Linda to rise.

"One of many workdays."

Ellie chuckled.

"Oh, yes, many, so very many! We'll start this one with cinnamon rolls!"

Maddy smiled, and, leading Linda, followed Ellie into the house.

NATHAN DROVE HIS BLUE pickup south from Roandale toward the turnoff to the Davis farm. He and Jason planned to meet at Ellie's place since Jason would be driving from his home located in the opposite direction, closer to the Fish and Wildlife Service office.

As the paved road heading east toward the farm came into view, Nathan slowed the truck. Recalling the large log house, the big greenhouse, the stream, and the vineyard, memories of times with Ellie's grandfather flashed through his brain. The older man's excitement over the greenhouse and vineyard had been gratifying and contagious.

"This is going to help so much! I appreciate you, Nathan, for taking your weekend to help me get this up. I'll have an extra crop of vegetables before summer even begins!"

"Glad to help, Cal. You know you're going to be busy with the increased number of tourists expected this year."

"Yep, but my girl Ellie will be here more often. She got a transfer to Glacier two months ago. She comes to see Marie and me a few times a week now — at least when the late winter weather cooperates, and the roads are open. This summer she intends to stay with us during her days off."

"I look forward to meeting her"

Cal's grin had stretched farther across his face.

"I think the two of you would make a great couple — you got lots in common. Last time you were here, you told me you didn't have a girlfriend any longer — that still true?"

"Now, Cal, don't go trying to set me up with your granddaughter. I have things going on in my life right now that I have to take care of, and getting over Ashley is one of them."

Now, as his pickup meandered toward the farm's driveway, Nathan thought, *If Cal had lived longer, I'd have taken him up on that set-up with his granddaughter. I wonder what he would think of us now?*

CHAPTER 19

Ellie admired Nathan's work ethic as the two of them spent time in the vineyard that morning. She also admired his physique. The red T-shirt rippled as his upper arms worked to dig out a broken water pipe. A black outline of a mountain, etched across the center of the front and back of the shirt, moved as Nathan's muscles strained to loosen a stubborn piece of the broken water system. His biceps rose and fell like ocean waves as he dug into the dirt. He leaned at the waist, and his hands hauled out the items determined to not be replaced.

"There!"

Nathan held up his prize like a triumphant gold medalist.

Ellie smiled.

"Stubborn little guy."

"I might not have buried it deep enough, but it sure decided to give me a run for my money getting it out of the ground," Nathan responded. "Would you hand me that hand rake? I need to loosen up some more dirt so the replacement valve won't try to hibernate like this one."

Ellie gave him the claw-like digging tool, and in a few moments, she handed him the new valve, black rubber pipe, and spicket. He attached all the items and then, using the gardening trowel, covered them with the enriched earth.

"Last one done," Nathan said.

He stood, looked at Ellie, and grinned.

"What did I hear earlier about cinnamon rolls?" he asked.

She smiled.

"I think you've earned one or two. Maybe some water first, though, uh?"

As she picked up one of two stainless steel water bottles, Nathan replied, "Yeah, that sounds good."

She handed him a gray one, and he uncapped it.

"Thanks. By the way, those paintings Maddy's already created are incredible! She's talented."

After taking a drink from the second bottle, a rose-colored thermos, Ellie responded, "She certainly is. I know she was concerned about losing her talent, but in just a few days, she's found motivation and inspiration again."

Nathan drank a bit more from the gray bottle and asked, "Why was she concerned?"

"Long story but the short version is boyfriend trouble."

"Oh. So she has a boyfriend. Jason will be disappointed."

After a quick smile to Nathan, Ellie said, "Former boyfriend. She broke up with him."

Nathan's eyes widened.

"That's good news for Jason."

"Maddy's not here to hook up with a guy again, not now at least. She's here to heal, get back to her art, and help me."

As he began picking up the scattered tools, Nathan said, "Well, her art is really good, and I'm glad she's been inspired already."

"I plan to display her work at the gazebo for the open house we're planning, and I hope she'll be able to show and even sell at some of the local galleries before summer ends."

Nathan looked at her.

"You really care about her, don't you?"

Ellie looked at him.

"Of course. She's family."

Ellie piled pieces of old pipe at the end of a row of grape vines.

"I'm going to do a test run with the system later this afternoon," she said.

"Why don't you do it over lunch? That way, if we find a spot we missed, we'll know it now and I can pick up more parts if needed yet today or at least tomorrow. I'm out of town most of next week working at Sweeney."

"Do you have a special project over there?"

"Training the seasonal range specialist and biologist. I'm hoping now that we have additional cranes in the valley here, I'll get those two up to speed over there by the end of the week and won't have to make as many trips as I did last summer. I'd like to help Jason with the crane observations as much as possible. And of course, if you keep seeing one or two over here, well, I'd just have to make some trips this way as well."

His flirty smile made Ellie's knees weak.

What have I gotten myself into?

Although fear tried to create a vice around her heart, the pleasant feelings of attraction, appreciation, and admiration took deeper root. She secretly reminded herself Nathan was not Grant nor her father. Perhaps it was time to trust a man again, like she had trusted her Grandad.

He and Grandad were friends, and they did help each other.

"You okay, Ellie?"

His question interrupted her thoughts.

She smiled and said, "Yeah, just thinking for a moment. I would hope you'd be here more often than over there. For a biologist that enjoys studying sandhill cranes, spending your work hours in a valley without cranes doesn't make sense. Besides, there are certain benefits a certain biologist receives at the Davis Family Farm."

Nathan leaned on a long-handled shovel he picked up earlier, and he looked at her.

"Oh really? And what might some of those be?"

"Hmm," Ellie said, tapping her index finger on her chin. "I'm trying to remember. Oh, yes, cinnamon rolls."

She grinned. Nathan returned her smile. He extended his right hand, and with his thumb, rubbed her chin.

"You've got some dirt ..."

He laughed and said, "I think I made it worse. My hands are dirtier and now, so is your face."

Ellie's eyes locked onto his, and her hand closed over his. She then looked at his hands, large and tanned. She rubbed her thumb over his knuckles and upon his palm. She then interlocked the fingers of their hands and returned her gaze to his face. She stood on tiptoes and leaned her face toward him. Her lips touched his in a light, sweet kiss.

NATHAN RELISHED THE feathery brush of her lips. Eyes closed, he savored the sensations her touch caused physically and emotionally. After the kiss, Ellie laid her head on his chest, and he enveloped her in his arms.

"I'm scared, Nathan," she whispered. "Feelings I haven't felt in years and experiences I haven't allowed myself to enjoy take hold when I'm around you, and it all scares the daylights out of me."

"I understand," he said in a soothing voice, as his hand caressed her back. "I think it's okay to be scared."

He took a deep breath and continued, "The last relationship I had burned me, and I've been hesitant to get involved with anyone since then. Haven't really dated, for that matter. But being with you, sharing things with you, learning more about you, well, I ... I want to step into that possibility again."

He took a slight step back and looked into her eyes.

"We can be scared together," Nathan whispered.

He searched her face and savored the smoothness of her cheeks and glint in her olive eyes. Nathan bent his head. His lips captured hers in a gentle, yet ardent kiss.

A moment later, as he held her again, Ellie said, "I want that, too. Being scared together sounds like a safe place."

He took a short step back and smiled at her. Then he said, "Did I hear something about cinnamon rolls?"

Her chuckle warmed his heart, and he joined in the low laughter.

CHAPTER 20

That evening, Ellie and Maddy walked through the doorway of the Shoreliner Saloon, Ellie leading the way. She nearly jumped when a familiar, rich baritone voice, coming from behind her, said, "Pretty packed in here tonight."

She turned around to see Nathan's smiling face.

"Do you like sneaking up on people?"

She tried to make her voice convey annoyance. But it was Nathan after all, and the dashing smile remained.

"Yeah, it's pretty fun. Almost as much fun as you have startling cranes."

"Ha, ha."

Nathan shifted his stance, giving Maddy opportunity to stand closer.

"Hey, Madison — good to see you again."

"Yeah, you, too. It's been a while."

She grinned at him.

"Jason and I grabbed a table over by the window, giving a view of the lake. The place is filling up."

"Sure is. But I expected that with Continental Divide playing," Ellie said.

"We did, too, that's why we came earlier."

He tilted his head toward the right.

"Follow me, ladies."

Ellie and Madison fell in step behind Nathan as he led the way to the table on the right side of the bar. Ellie saw Jason at a table set for four, a glass of beer in front of him. When the three drew near, Jason stood up. Ellie noticed he kept his eyes on Madison, and she hid a smile. His attraction toward Maddy was totally apparent; she hoped Madison would be kind.

"Hey, Madison. Hi, Ellie," he greeted. "Long time no see."

His teasing voice and flirting grin brought a smile to Ellie's face. She glanced at Maddy, who was also smiling.

"I just said the same to Nathan," Maddy stated.

"Great minds think alike," replied Jason, as he pulled out a chair next to him.

He indicated the chair was for Maddy, who complied and sat down.

Nathan pulled out a chair on the opposite side of Maddy and bowed toward Ellie.

"My lady," he said.

She grinned.

"Thank you."

Nathan took the chair next to her. A nearby window provided a view of the sun set.

"Gorgeous sky this evening," Nathan said.

Ellie glanced at him and then at the view. Snow still topped the surrounding mountains, and hints of rose and apricot bathed the peaks in alpine glow.

"I love this time of the evening," she said.

"It's truly beautiful," Maddy commented.

"Sunsets are a reason I enjoy living here," Jason chimed in.

"The server brought menus so we can order anytime," Nathan said.

Ellie took the one he handed to her with a 'thank you,' and she began to peruse the plastic-coated list.

"I haven't been here in a few years. Anything in particular you like?"

Ellie directed her question to Nathan but also glanced at Jason.

"I'm partial to the ribs," the younger man said, glancing at her.

"It's been a while since I've been here as well," Nathan stated. "I'm more into the Italian selections."

"They cut back on those," Jason said.

"Ah, but they still have my favorite."

"And what's that?" Ellie asked.

"Chicken marsala."

Her eyebrows raised.

"Mine, too."

Nathan smiled at her.

"What about you, Maddy?" Jason asked, looking at Ellie's cousin.

"I'm a Mexican menu kind of girl."

"One of the chefs here is Hispanic. She makes a mean salsa, and the enchiladas are really good."

"Then, I guess that's what I'm having. I wasn't sure there would be good Mexican food up here."

"The Shoreliner is a premier eating establishment, especially for this area," Jason informed her. "It's a hopping place in the summer when tourists come, but it's also popular with local folks."

"How'd you come to know so much about the place? I thought you've only lived here a year or so."

"I once dated the owner."

Surprise registered on Madison's face, and Ellie was sure her expression indicated the same.

Jason shrugged.

"Free food and half-price drinks. Wasn't a bad gig."

Madison shook her head and gazed at Ellie. Hand to her cheek, Maddy mouthed to Ellie, "For real?"

"WELL, AT LEAST WE KNOW the food's good."

Nathan's statement hinted at his nervousness regarding the direction of the conversation. Ellie seemed to notice for she steered to a different topic.

"So, tell me more about the lab, River. She sounds lovely."

Nathan smiled.

"Oh, she is! Completely trained, sweet, laid-back. How would you describe her, Jason?"

"I only met the dog once, but yeah, those qualities for sure. I'd add smart, too. I think Angie said she did dock diving and hunting trials with River in the past."

"Did you date her, too?" Maddy quipped.

"No. I don't date co-workers," Jason said.

"Oh, so you do have some ethics."

"Yes, I have a code – no dating co-workers. Can get messy. Been there, done that, and it wasn't pretty."

"Of course," Maddy murmured.

Nathan rolled his eyes. This time he maneuvered the boat of conversation.

"Seems like Linda and the two cats are getting along there at your place."

He looked from Ellie to Madison and back again.

Ellie nodded.

"They are all doing great. The cats have really taken to Maddy."

"What can I say – I'm a cat lady. Always have been, always will be."

"I miss having pets," Nathan said. "The job just keeps me too busy."

Ellie looked at Jason.

"What about you, Jason? Dogs, cats, horses – any pets at home or while growing up?"

"Had a raccoon once and a squirrel – that's what got me into wildlife management. Both were orphans, and my dad and I brought them home. My two brothers and I raised them, but Mom wasn't too keen on keeping them, especially once they started raiding the garbage and her pantry."

"What happened to them?"

Ellie voiced the question Nathan wondered but felt reluctant to ask.

"There was a wildlife rehabilitation center and sanctuary the next county over – we took them there. I'd visit occasionally when my dad or mom would drive me."

"So that's what got you into the line of work you do now?" Ellie asked.

Jason nodded.

"That's a nice story," Maddy commented. "You rescued wildlife, and Ellie and I rescue pets and livestock."

"Yeah, so when do the other animals arrive at the farm? You were saying something about that earlier today," Jason said.

Nathan looked at Ellie and she at him. Under the table, he reached over and took one of her hands. The warmth he experienced helped him relax.

"Chickens on Monday," Ellie responded. "Lambs on Wednesday, and the mini-donkeys and the goats in about a week."

She looked at Nathan.

"So, Maddy and I think we should meet River. She sounds like a nice fit for our little family, and we decided it's not too soon to have Linda meet a new potential friend. Can you set that up for us?"

"Sure," Nathan responded. "Want to try for tomorrow afternoon?"

"My mother is visiting tomorrow. Any evening next week, though."

"I'll be out of town, remember? But, I don't have to be there. I can text Angie, give her your number, and the two of you can set a day and time. Will that work?"

Ellie nodded and squeezed his hand. The server arrived, and Nathan unlocked his fingers from Ellie's. He then texted Angie as his companions placed their dinner order.

CHAPTER 21

Two hours later, dinner plates cleared from the saloon's tables, the crowd began chanting for the band. Ellie turned in her chair to get a better look at the stage. Nathan stood.

"Here, let's move our chairs so we can see."

As Ellie rose to her five-foot-six-inch height, she heard the rustle of metal against the wooden floor as others in the establishment relocated their chairs to view the stage.

"Much better," Nathan stated.

They sat down again, and Ellie nodded her thanks to him.

The stage began filling with musicians. The audience clapped and cheered. Cowboy hats adorned the performers' heads as each band member, five in all, walked toward the microphones. The woman went to the keyboards. One man picked up a bass. Another walked to the drum set, while the other two men chose a guitar and banjo, respectively.

The lead singer, holding the banjo, smiled at the crowd.

"Hey, there, Paradise, Montana! We're so happy to be with you all. Who's ready for some music and dancing?"

The crowd, including Ellie, Nathan, and Jason, cheered. Maddy remained quiet. Ellie glanced at her for a moment and raised her eyebrows. Maddy shrugged.

Ellie returned her eyes to the stage. The music began, a fast country-rock song, and people began gathering on the dance floor. Ellie felt a touch upon her elbow. She looked over at Nathan, and he nodded toward the scene.

"Wanna give it a go?"

She smiled.

"Love to!"

She rose from her chair, and Nathan did the same. Hand on her elbow, he guided her to the dance floor. He grinned at her, and they began to dance.

At first shimmying with some distance between them, Nathan and Ellie incorporated jazz hands and swimming arms with their dance steps. A few minutes into the song, they drew closer together. Ellie's dark hair glimmered in the saloon's dim lights, like the sun's rays bouncing off the lake, Nathan thought. Her southwestern-patterned skirt swayed as her hips and legs moved. Her gracefulness, and the joy exhibited on her face, made him smile. He drew closer, took her right hand, and swung her under his left arm, country-swing style. Ellie laughed.

Too soon, the song ended, but they stayed on the dance floor as another fast number began. This time, Nathan kept Ellie's hand in his and they two-stepped on the wooden floor.

"You're good at this," he whispered into her ear.

She smiled.

"You're not so bad yourself."

"Thank you. It's been a while, but, like a bicycle, I guess you don't forget once you get back into it."

They danced apart for a short time, and then Nathan drew her in close for two more twirls. She placed her hand on his shoulder, and they fast-waltzed for a bit.

"I imagine work keeps you busy," Ellie commented.

Nathan nodded.

"It does that, yeah. But I also don't frequent bars often anymore. I used to have a tendency to drink too much, and I don't want to go down that road again."

"It's amazing the difference between being twenty-two and thirty-two," she replied.

"I take it you traveled that same road when you were younger?"

She nodded.

"Yeah. Wised up and made the same decision as you."

"Well, I'm glad you came out tonight."

She smiled.

"When you told me who was playing, how could I say 'no'?"

"I thought it was because I promised I wouldn't step on your toes."

She grinned.

"That too."

They began to two-step. Ellie, more confident, fell into the tempo of the music and Nathan's dancing style. Ellie smiled. The music freed her. A new life at the farm, a helper in her cousin, animals for which to care, and plants to grow and sell. And now a man with whom to spend time with who promised to work alongside her. Someone she had much in common with, including a respect for her grandparents. Ellie felt happiness flow through her as steady as the guitar player's rhythmic strum.

Nathan took her hand again and twirled her twice. Their eyes met. His, smokey gray in the dim lighting, twinkled. He smiled at her. Ellie believed he, too, was enjoying the music and dancing.

The tune slowed. Nathan enfolded Ellie into his arms, moving from two-step to a waltz-like sway.

The lead singer said, "Alright, folks, time to slow it down a bit. Time to get close."

A woman's voice behind Nathan intruded on the slow dance.

"Hey, handsome, how about waltzing with me?"

OF ALL PEOPLE!

Nathan grimaced. His eyes left Ellie's lovely face. He turned his head and acknowledged her with a nod.

"Ashley."

She pursed her lips, bright with red lipstick, and her chocolate eyes danced with mischief.

"You've been missing from this scene a long time, cowboy," she quipped. "Kind of surprised to see you here."

Ashley looked at Ellie and held out her hand.

"Ashley Kramer – I'm an associate realtor here in the valley. I don't think I've seen you before. New to the area? In need of a place to buy or rent?"

Inwardly, Nathan groaned.

"She's not in the market for property, Ashley."

The young woman shrugged as she and Ellie shook hands.

"Oh, well, if you ever are, I'm your girl," rambled Ashley. "Born and raised in the valley so I know every inch of this area. I helped Nathan get his place in Roandale. By the way, I didn't catch your name."

Why now? Why anytime? And twice in the past two days?

Nathan's heart raced.

CHAPTER 22

Ellie looked at the black-haired, slender intruder. She had felt the magnetic pull between she and Nathan, but now detected a tension between the woman standing across from her and the man she knew she was starting to fall for.

As she shook Ashley's hand, Ellie said, "I'm Eleanor Davis, Ellie Davis."

Ashley's dark brown eyes widened.

"Cal Davis' granddaughter?"

"Yes. You knew my grandfather?"

Ashley shook her head.

"Never met him but certainly knew of him. Especially through your father."

Ellie frowned.

"My father?"

"Ladies, why don't we move this conversation off the dance floor? We're blocking people."

As she followed Nathan and Ashley closer the bar, Ellie thought, *How would Dad have encountered this woman who hadn't known Grandad?*

Standing near a large beam in the middle of the building, Ashley responded to the unasked question.

"After your grandfather died, your dad contacted me to sell the property."

"He did?"

The realtor's bright red lips smiled.

"The lead agent and I were to take the listing originally after your grandfather's death. You're sitting on a mint, you know, Miss Davis."

"Ashley."

Nathan's voice undergirded an authoritative warning. Ellie looked at him.

"How long have you two known each other?"

Ellie directed the question to Nathan, but Ashley responded, honey dripping from her voice.

"We met when Nathan arrived in the valley. As I said, I helped him buy his house. We became an item and were for quite a long time, actually."

Ellie looked from one to another.

"I see," she said quietly.

"That was some time ago," Nathan said.

"Not that long ago."

Ellie looked at Ashley.

"I see," she said again.

Ashley's brown eyes grew wide once again.

"Oh, the two of you..."

"Are friends," Ellie interrupted. "He helped my grandfather with some projects."

"Yes, I know," Ashley stated. "The greenhouse and vineyard added a lot of value to the property. When your dad talked to me again in January ..."

"He did what?"

Ellie voice boomed with shock and bitterness.

"Ellie, please..."

She looked at Nathan and her eyes narrowed.

"You stay out of this."

She looked at Ashley.

"He approached you in January?"

The woman, apparently taken aback, nodded, and she glanced from Ellie to Nathan and back again.

"He said he thought he'd have the property back by February and that he wanted to sell. A few weeks later, he called and said it didn't work out in his favor and so the deal was off."

"Excuse me."

Ellie walked to the table where Madison still sat. She had moved across the table from Jason, occupying Ellie's former seat. Ellie leaned down and whispered into Maddy's ear, "Let's go. I need to get out of here."

"What? Why? You looked like you were having a good time."

"Let's just go. I know you're not really enjoying yourself, and frankly, I've lost interest in staying."

Ellie grabbed her jacket from the chair and began walking toward the door. Nathan caught her arm. She glared at him.

"Ellie, don't go. There are things we should talk about," he said.

"I'm not feeling very social right now. I have things to think about."

"Ellie, please. Let's talk."

"Talk to Ashley. It's apparent she's eager to have you back."

She broke free and reached the door. Maddy caught up with her.

"What's going on?"

"I'll tell you in the car."

NATHAN SIGHED AS ELLIE left the saloon. His shoulders sagged as he walked toward the table, Jason's eyes watching him. Ashley caught his arm.

"Hey, come dance with me."

He turned and glared at her.

"I think you've done enough damage."

Her eyes narrowed.

"What are you talking about?"

"Never mind. Just go, Ashley."

Nathan sat down and put his head in his hands.

"Who, her? You're upset over the old man's granddaughter?"

Nathan looked up and glared at the woman he once thought he loved.

"I told you – that man had a name. And he was a decent guy, a great guy. And his granddaughter ... well, she's a lot like him – good and decent."

Ashley placed her hands on her hips.

"So, you are with her tonight."

"I was. Until you came along. Just go, Ashley."

Instead, she leaned over and placed her lips next to his ear.

"Come on, Nathan. We had a good thing going. We can pick up where we left off. She's a farm girl, granted she might be a wealthy farm girl, but you know I have a lucrative career. So do you. Together, you and I are unstoppable."

Nathan lifted his head. His gray eyes clouded over as he looked into her dark brown ones.

"We broke up for a reason, and there's no way we're getting back together. I don't want to be with you, Ashley."

Nathan turned away, and Ashley straightened to her five-foot-eight frame. Hands on her hips, she glared at him.

"Well, I'll have you know, Nathan Ford, you're not the only man in this valley. I've had plenty of dates, and more than one guy in my life, since you and I broke up. I do not need you."

"Good. Now just leave me alone."

He heard her high heels click on the floor as she stalked away.

After a moment, Jason whispered, "Dude – what happened?"

"Ashley happened, that's what happened."

Nathan groaned.

"Just when I thought I'd open my heart again, my ex blows in like a hurricane and ruins it. Ellie will likely not speak to me again. I thought something else might ruin us, but no, it has to the real estate witchdoctor."

CHAPTER 23

Ellie sat on the loveseat inside the living room, and she skimmed the visitor's guide she had picked up from a rack at the airport the day Madison arrived. A cup of lavender-chamomile tea steeped on the table next to her, and a mug of mint tea awaited Madison. She gazed at the fire burning in the woodstove that stood in the corner of the living room. Flames flickered with intensity, taking the chill off the late-night air. Grammy's cuckoo clock, which arrived with her ancestors from Scandinavia more than 100 years before, chimed once, reminding Ellie it was Sunday morning.

I should have been in bed hours ago.

Ellie sighed.

"This will be a short night," she whispered.

"For all of us."

Maddy, in her fleece lounging outfit, fell into the nearby recliner.

"Your tea's ready," Ellie said in a soft voice.

"Thanks. I'll get it in a minute."

Her cousin's sullen attitude echoed through the room.

"So, what's going on with you tonight? My night ended pretty awful, but yours seemed to start off that way."

Maddy sighed.

"I wanted to have fun, I really did, but that guy Jason — he rubs me the wrong way."

"I could tell. So could everyone else around you. Listen, I know he comes across arrogant ..."

"Oh, he *is* arrogant."

Ellie sighed.

"I guess neither of us were happy tonight."

Maddy studied her.

"Really? You and Nathan seemed to be enjoying yourselves on the dance floor. This is, until that woman showed up."

Ellie nodded.

"Yeah, between her being Nathan's former girlfriend and Dad's co-schemer in taking the farm away from me, I wasn't skipping down the yellow brick road anymore."

She shook her head.

"I just need to stick to my original plan and stay on the farm, focusing all my attention and energy into making this a lucrative business."

"We both do," Maddy stated. "I was hoping that, spending some time out with a guy, even as a new friend and among other friends, I'd keep the past in the past, but I guess this break-up with Stewart continues to haunt me."

"We've all been hurt, in one way or another, with relationships," Ellie said. "Me with my Dad, me with Grant, you and your dad, you and Stewart, heck, our own mothers didn't choose wisely."

Maddy gave Ellie a quick smile.

"Yeah, that's for sure. But the music tonight was great, that's one positive thing about the evening."

Ellie also smiled.

"Wasn't it? They're a great band. And the food was pretty good."

Maddy grinned.

"Well, at least arrogant Jason didn't steer us wrong about that."

"Maybe dating a chef or the owner of a place like the Shoreliner isn't 'a bad gig,' as Jason called it!"

Ellie and Maddy laughed.

"Okay, so my mother is visiting tomorrow," Ellie said. "I've been looking over this visitor's guide, and I'd like your input. Where should we go that you would enjoy and that mother would like?"

"I still need some canvases and easels. What do you suggest?"

Ellie handed the guide to Maddy and said, "Look through this at breakfast. You'll probably find some ideas."

Ellie took a sip of tea and then said, "You may not remember this, but the valley has some great art galleries. I know you love to paint, and so I thought you might like to visit some of the galleries and even take some time to spend on your artwork while you're here. There's a beautiful view of the valley and the Lincoln Mountains to the west, from an overlook above the farm. Maybe next week we can take some time and I'll show you the trail. You can go to the overlook when you want to do some painting."

Maddy smiled again. Ellie relaxed, as her cousin's sweet self seemed to return.

"That sounds great. I really want to get back into my art. I feel it's been an extremely long time since I've picked up a paint brush."

"You thought you'd be planning a wedding this summer, so I can see where your art would take a back seat for a time."

"Yeah, but it really was a big part of who I am. I miss that aspect of myself."

"We really can get ourselves twisted up in knots about guys, can't we?" Ellie commented and then sighed. "I thought I turned the page on that stuff a long time ago. Now look at me, upset over some woman Nathan used to date."

"Was it her and Nathan or the fact that your dad tried to steal the farm?"

"Both."

Ellie sighed again and began stroking Victor, who sat nearby. Linda lay at her feet, and Cecilia stood sentry next to Maddy.

"Nice to come home to these sweet creatures, isn't it?"

Ellie's question was necessarily directed at Maddy but served in its own way to soothe her aching, tattered heart.

"Yes, it certainly is. Look, Ellie, what your dad tried to do is horrible, really awful, but remember, it isn't Nathan's fault. Nathan's a man, yes, and men have hurt us, both of us, but Nathan isn't your dad, he isn't Grant, and he isn't Stewart. And he's not arrogant Jason. I think Nathan truly cares for you and not that real estate woman. Yes, they had a thing, but it's in the past. You've dated, and you had a serious relationship with Grant, but all that's in the past, too."

Ellie nodded.

"You're right. It's just all this came out of left field. Especially about Dad." She shook her head. "I just can't believe he tried to take the farm from me."

Tears came to her eyes.

"It hurts so much!"

Maddy reached over and patted Ellie's arm.

"I know, and I'm sorry. Being hurt really sucks, and when that hurt is caused by someone who's supposed to love us .... But it wasn't Nathan who hurt you."

Ellie nodded again.

"I was pretty mean, leaving like that."

"Just call him," Maddy said as she stood. "I'll give you some space."

Holding Cecilia, she padded down the hall in her slippers to her room and shut the door.

Ellie sighed and hugged Victor. She listened to his soothing purr for a moment, set him back on her lap, and then picked up her phone. She began to form a text and then erased it. She sighed. Victor leaped from her lap onto the back of the couch to watch the outdoors. Ellie stared out the window at the ink-like sky. She felt a paw upon her leg and glanced down. Linda's amber eyes stared into her face, and the dog's long muzzle lay upon her knee.

"Ah, sweetheart."

Ellie reached down and scratched the collie's soft head.

"You're pretty instinctual, aren't you? Like Grace."

She continued petting Linda and sighed again.

"I told Maddy I didn't want any distractions. Between my dad, this Ashley woman, and Nathan ... I think she has a thing for Nathan. Of course, who could blame her."

Her phone rang. She saw the ID and answered.

"Hey, there, Nathan."

"Hi. I'm sorry to call you so late. I was concerned. Are you doing okay?"

"Oh, I'm managing. Listen, I was thinking of calling you. I want to apologize ..."

"No need. Ashley was, is, a barracuda, and though she really doesn't know the story about your dad, she shouldn't have been so outspoken and hurtful. But that's just her. I want you to know, even though I used to be in a relationship with her, that was some time ago, and there is nothing between us now. At least not on my end."

"I appreciate knowing that. I was just taken by surprise, especially by the news about my dad's thoughts and intentions. I felt hurt."

"Yeah, I can understand. Listen, I know it's late, but can we go somewhere and talk? There are some things I want to share with you, and I'd prefer not to do it over the phone."

CHAPTER 24

Nathan stood at the front of his truck at the roadside picnic area along the Lake Lincoln shore. Located half-way between the Shoreliner Saloon and the Davis Family Farm, the pull-off consisted of two recycled wood picnic tables which stood on a ridge above the water's edge and a bear-proof metal garbage dumpster between them. Stars blinked and danced in the midnight sky, and Venus, Jupiter, and Mars cast their brightness as if in competition with their celestial neighbors.

Lights from a vehicle as it pulled off the highway caught his attention, and Nathan turned to see Ellie's Subaru drive toward him. She parked the vehicle to the right of his truck. He walked toward her as she opened the car door. He held it open as she exited the Forester.

"Thanks for meeting me."

"Grammy and I used to spend time here when I was younger," Ellie said. "It was always daylight though."

"It's a pretty spot in daytime or nighttime."

He took her elbow.

"Let's sit."

He guided her to the closest picnic table. She sat on the side facing the lake, and he took the bench opposite her.

"I again apologize for Ashley's behavior and her words."

"Why? None of it was your fault. I'm the one who should be sorry. I took things out on you that I shouldn't have. She ... She just caught me by surprise, especially about my dad."

Nathan nodded.

"I know. Me, too. I would never think a man was capable of being so conniving when it comes to family property and his own daughter."

"Well, the man loves money, what can I say? And he's never liked the farm. From what I understand, he couldn't wait to get away from the valley. I'm just so lucky he brought my brother and me to visit Grammy and Grandad on occasion and that, when I got older, I was able to stay most summers with them."

She shook her head and then said, "I don't understand how Dad could not love the farm or love it here in the valley."

She gazed upon the darkened lake and listened to the waves lap the shore. She then looked at the sky.

"It's so beautiful, peaceful and soothing" she whispered.

"I feel the same way."

Ellie looked at Nathan.

"When I arrived in Merritt Valley five years ago, I knew I'd come home," he said. "This community, this area, seemed just seemed to fill that part of me that wanted to stop moving around and plant roots."

"And Ashley?"

Nathan returned her gaze.

"There was a time I thought she and I ... that we'd be ... together and stay together. But her materialism and her push to build more, sell more, make more at the sacrifice of the natural beauty really turned me off. She had no interest in the work I did, just a feigned sense of attentiveness. I grew weary of our lack of common interests and the pretense."

"She's a gorgeous woman, a classy dresser with an esteemed career and an attractive body. I can see the two of you as the beautiful people of the valley."

He smiled slightly.

"Are you saying I'm handsome?"

"What do you think?"

Nathan placed his hands over Ellie's.

"Well, I think you're very beautiful, in more ways than one."

"Ashley is beautiful, and Madison is stunning. I'm nothing special."

"Eleanor Davis, don't ever let me hear you say that. You are special, you are beautiful, inside and out. Why do you think I'm so attracted to you? I know shallow and I know genuine, and you, lovely lady, are genuine. And that's the most beautiful of all."

Ellie sensed he might lean in and kiss her. However, he remained affixed to the bench. She squirmed in her seat, trying to quell the disappointment. Then, she looked at the night sky again and whispered, "Thank you for the compliment."

NATHAN DESIRED TO HOLD her in his arms and capture her lips with a deep kiss, securing his words with action. However, there was the matter he needed to share with her, and he had no idea if what he said would sever the connection he longed to deepen.

He spoke again, in a low voice.

"There's something I need to tell you, and it's crucial that you know because I don't want to keep any secrets from you, especially after what happened at the Shoreliner earlier."

Nathan drew a deep breath. He opened his mouth in an attempt to speak, but no words came forth. He looked heavenward, as if trying to draw strength and courage from the cosmos. How those stars and planets, the moon, even the sun remained suspended and didn't crash upon the earth was a wonder he always enjoyed pondering. The mysteries of nature, the tranquility of a forest, the soothing sounds of a waterway, the magnificence of an elk or a sandhill crane, the intricacies of a butterfly – each was a marvel, and, for Nathan, a joy.

His wondering mind returned to the present and his need to release his secret to her when Ellie asked, "You said on the phone you wanted to talk with me about something."

A sliver of fear shot through him. He stood and walked to the lakeshore. He stared at the water and began his confession.

"Two years ago, I was conducting bald eagle nest studies, and I took a fall, injuring my back. I was put on painkillers, and I ... I got addicted."

He took a deep breath and then turned to face Ellie. He remained where he stood as he continued, "I kept up a good front for several months, but it all finally caught up with me. I, uh, I checked myself into an in-house program with the encouragement of my supervisor, and when I got out, your grandfather had passed. I learned he had paid a few months of my mortgage. I was dumbfounded that Cal would do such a thing for someone not related to him."

"Wait. An addiction? Recovery? Grandad?"

"Yeah. I know it's a lot to take in, and it's not something I'm proud of."

Ellie looked away.

"I'm clean now and have been for the last six months. Like I said, not something I'm proud of."

"Well, you should be."

He stared at her. She returned his gaze and said, "I mean, not the addiction itself, but the courage and strength to admit you had a problem and you needed help. I've known a few people who lived in denial, whether it was an alcohol addiction, food addiction, or drug addiction. You're a man of integrity, Nathan, professionally and personally."

"You're okay knowing this about me? That I'm a recovering opioid addict?"

Ellie stood.

"I admit that I'm surprised, but Nathan, that part of your life, the addiction, is in the past, and as long as it's in the past, then, yes, I'm fine."

She took a step toward him, adding, "Everyone has issues and struggles, things they deal with. I have a father I can barely stand to be around, especially after learning what I did tonight. If you can be okay with the drama in my family, knowing I stay away from my parents as much as possible, then I can be okay with your recovery ... and help you continue that journey."

Nathan smiled.

"And what about your grandfather helping pay my mortgage? I didn't ask him ..."

Ellie shrugged.

"That's my Grandad. He helped people when they needed it – that was who he was. I know of many people who benefited from his generosity. I'm one of them. So, no, I have no problem with that either."

Nathan took one large step and stood in front of Ellie.

"You're an amazing woman, Eleanor Davis."

Nathan leaned toward her. She placed her hands on his chest.

"I just have a few questions."

"Sure. What?"

He heard her intake of breath and dropped her hands from his body.

"You're being totally straight with me, right? No drugs?"

"No drugs. I wouldn't have a job if I was still on them."

She nodded and then asked, "And you and Ashley – that is the past, too, right?"

He nodded and then clasped her hands in his.

"Totally," he whispered. "My heart belongs to you."

He leaned in, placing his forehead against hers.

"I'm falling hard for you, Ellie." He took a deep breath and then said, "I know we haven't known each other very long, but yet, in a way, I feel like I've known you a long time. Cal spoke fondly of you in the years I knew him. So did Marie."

He stepped back slightly to look into her face.

"I was scared how you might react to the news of my former addiction. You have your grandfather's heart, and for that, I'm grateful."

He felt a smile come to her face.

"I'm pleased you think that – he was a fine, fine man. Like I told you, Nathan, everyone makes mistakes. You know the struggles I have with my dad, and then to learn tonight he nearly filed a lawsuit to get the property ... There's a lot of ugliness in my family line."

Nathan stepped back and nodded.

"I can handle that. After all, I'm on your side, just as I was on Cal's side."

"Thank you for being such a good friend to my Grandad. That means a lot to me."

"He meant a lot to me. You mean a lot to me."

Nathan placed a gentle kiss upon her lips. A shiver of excitement coursed through him as she responded.

Afterward, with a smile, he held her hand and said, "Since we didn't get to waltz at the Shoreliner, let's waltz along the shore."

Ellie smiled at his invitation. As their bodies came together and their hands locked, Nathan relished the embrace, and they began to sway to their own music. A few moments later, Ellie stepped out of his arms

"Since you shared something important with me, I think I should do the same."

Nathan placed a finger upon her lips.

"Whatever it is, it can wait. We've had a lot come at us tonight. Let's just enjoy the quiet, alone time we have right now. We can talk more later."

"But ..." she mumbled.

He smiled and then captured her lips with his with another kiss. This time, however, he poured his desire into the embrace, and discovered her hunger for him in return as she wrapped her arms around his neck and deepened the kiss.

CHAPTER 25

Mid-morning the following day, Ellie, her mother, and Maddy walked Roandale's downtown boardwalk. Sunlight showered the small community near Lincoln Lake, the largest body of water in the Merritt Valley, and many shop doors opened to let in the warmth and light.

Each woman carried a bag, Maddy's the largest, containing two canvases and three paint brushes. A large grin graced her face.

"I'm excited that my creativity has returned! I've been so stale the past several months, but this area is reinvigorating me," she said.

"I'm glad to hear that, dear," Julie Davis said. "You're so talented! I need more Maddy paintings on my walls at home."

"And we need some at the farmhouse," Ellie replied. "And for the vineyard gazebo, especially with the Memorial weekend open house coming up."

"I don't think I can get too many more paintings created by then," Maddy stated. "It's only a few weeks away."

"We'll display the ones you've done and a few from the grandparents' collection," Ellie said. "You know they have several from your show in Missoula five years ago."

"Those are old. I'm a different artisan than I was then. People need to see what I do now."

"We have the landscapes you've already painted, and with the creations at my grandparents' we'll tell people they're 'a taste' of your talent. We can schedule an actual show for later in the summer."

"That sounds like a good plan," Ellie's mother said. "Maybe you can leave some with Ellie before you return to school and she can have a harvest time event, which includes sales of the paintings you create while you're in the valley. I'm sure the money will help for your last year of your master's program."

"You're right, Aunt Julie – it would," Maddy replied.

As they passed another craft and gift shop, Maddy said, "Oh! I need to dash in here for a minute. Either of you ladies want to go in with me?"

Ellie and Julie shook their heads.

"Go on – we'll wait out here," Ellie stated.

"I'll be right back!"

Maddy darted inside.

"I've heard that before," Ellie commented quietly.

A black iron and wooden bench stood near the doorway. Ellie indicated for her mother to sit, and she took a seat beside her.

"Mom," Ellie began. "I need to tell you something I learned last night."

"What's that, dear?"

"It's about dad – and him wanting to sell the farm."

"What about it? That was last year. I thought you'd put that behind you since your grandfather's will specifically stated you inherited the property."

"Yeah, well, apparently dad was ready to fight that in court."

Julie looked at Ellie.

"What? Who told you that?"

"A local real estate person. She said Dad told her in January he had a plan to get the farm back and that when he did, he would sell it, hiring her agency to list the property."

"No, that can't be."

Ellie studied her mother's face, which registered shock from her eyes to her forehead.

"Surely the agent heard wrong," Julie stated.

Ellie shrugged.

"Well, if she did, it was a multi-million-dollar misunderstanding. She also told me Dad called her back in February and said he wasn't going to get the land back in his possession, and so the real estate listing wouldn't happen. You're sure you never heard him say anything?"

Her mother nodded.

"I'm very sure. I would have disowned him if he tried to steal the property from you."

Julie laid her hand upon Ellie's arm.

"Honey, this whole thing has been a nightmare for me. Your own father treated his parents shamefully, and when I realized the extent to which his desire for money went, I warned him to not do anything to further jeopardize our family relationships. I'm very happy you and your grandparents were so close – with my own parents gone since you were small, your dad's parents were the only granny and grandad you really knew. That relationship was, and remains, special. I'm really sorry your father turned out as he did."

"You mean since I was pregnant."

"Well, that didn't help matters when it came to him, but no, even before, when you didn't follow his advice to major in business in college. You chose what you wanted to do, not what he wanted you to do, and though you followed your heart, that decision crushed him."

"Made him mad, you mean."

"Hurt his pride, really."

"But Eric majored in business and now works for that big company in Spokane."

"Pacific Paper Products."

Ellie nodded.

"Yes, but you're the firstborn," Julie said. "He wanted you to follow in his footsteps even more so than he wanted Eric to."

Ellie shook her head.

"I'll never understand why he just wouldn't accept that's not who I am. Why am I supposed to be like him anyway? I'm good at what I do, and I loved my work with the Park Service."

Her mother smiled.

"Eleanor, parents want what's best for their children. Someday, you'll know that feeling."

Ellie stared at her mother.

"I do know that feeling, Mom," she whispered. "I may not be raising Kevin, but I do want what's best for him. And that includes what makes him happy. He doesn't have to work for the Park Service, or do anything in the outdoors, for me to love him. Why couldn't Dad just want me to be happy, in my work, in my relationships? I feel like he's betrayed me, more than once. How can I have a relationship with someone, with my father, when he betrays me?"

At that moment, Maddy slipped out the shop door, another package of purchases in her hand.

"Sketching paper! I remembered reading about this place in the visitor guide Ellie picked up for me. They sell some incredible art paper, including sketch pads. I got the last two on the shelf."

Ellie smiled at her cousin's enthusiasm.

"That's what I mean, Mom. I love Maddy for who she is and her excitement about what she does."

Maddy looked at Ellie.

"What? What are you talking about."

"Never mind," Ellie said, and she stood up.

She did so without looking and bumped into someone walking by.

"Excuse me," came a familiar masculine voice.

She turned to look into Nathan's handsome face.

NATHAN PUT HIS HAND out to steady himself and then smiled when he saw Ellie.

"Interesting seeing you in the community where I live. I didn't know you were coming or I'd have offered to buy you lunch."

"This is one of the best local communities for shopping," Ellie replied. "Maddy wanted some new art supplies."

Nathan noticed the two large bags in Maddy's hand. The smile remained on his face.

"Looks like she found some, too."

He noticed an auburn-haired woman stand from the bench and position herself beside Ellie. The lady was finely-dressed, wearing sleek ivory pants and a shimmering pale pink and yellow blouse. The woman's face was lovely, almost mirroring Ellie's features, yet more slender. He noted their eyes were the same olive-color.

"Mom, this is Nathan Ford," Ellie said. "He's the supervisory biologist for the Merritt Valley Wildlife Refuge as well as the Sweeney River Refuge on the other side of the mountain range. Nathan, this is my mother, Julie Davis. She lives in Missoula and is visiting Maddy and me for the day."

"Oh, right – I remember now you mentioned that," Nathan said as he looked from Ellie to her mother. He held out his hand.

"Mrs. Davis – so very nice to meet you."

"You as well. And you two know each other how?"

"Sandhill cranes."

Ellie and Nathan spoke simultaneously then looked at each other and laughed.

"Umm – I'm not sure I understand," Julie stated.

"It's obvious – they're nature lovers. They bonded over birds and the great outdoors," Maddy said. "And they look really great dancing together."

"I see," Mrs. Davis said. "Dancing, uh?"

Nathan noticed the blush that crept up Ellie's neck. He wondered if his face was also turning red as he experienced a slight heat rising from the back of his head.

"I knew Mr. Davis ... Cal," Nathan said. "I helped build the greenhouse and establish the vineyard. I also bought produce from him a lot. When I met your daughter at the wildlife refuge a while ago, well, I remembered Cal talking about her, Marie, too, for that matter."

He glanced at Ellie. Despite the hardware store bag in his hand, he felt the desire to put an arm around Ellie's waist. However, he refrained.

"Anyway, with our similar backgrounds, Ellie and I ... well, she and I ... we just hit it off."

"'Hit it off?'"

"We're dating, Mom, okay? Yes, I'm finally dating again. Gee, can you not make a big deal about it?"

Ellie's outburst took Nathan aback. He looked at her again.

"Well, I think it's a pretty big deal. I thought we were enjoying spending time together."

"We are. I am."

"It's just that Ellie hasn't really dated anyone since Kevin was born. Well, actually, since she and Grant broke up."

"Mom!"

"Oh, boy," Maddy whispered and turned away from the group.

Nathan looked from Ellie to her mother.

"Kevin? Grant?"

Nathan's short questions and glances created a tension as thick as the early spring valley fog.

"I'm confused," Nathan confessed. "Who is Kevin and who is Grant?"

"Her son and her son's father. She hasn't told you?"

Mrs. Davis looked intently at Nathan and then at Ellie.

"You haven't told him?"

"The time hasn't been right. I've been meaning to," Ellie said.

Nathan looked at her as his stomach knotted. Ellie's glare at her mother made his insides flip.

"Excuse me," he whispered.

Nathan began to walk away. He heard Ellie call his name, but he continued walking.

CHAPTER 26

Ellie ran the boardwalk to catch up with Nathan. Her brown leather boots seemed to echo each time her foot hit the wooden walkway. Anger at her mother welled up like steam, and Nathan's reaction, his walking away from her, churned that vapor into a boil.

"Nathan! Stop! Let's talk about this."

He ignored her.

"Nathan! Wait!"

She focused on him and not on people's stares. Finally, he paused, and then he turned around.

"Talk about what? That you have a child I haven't met?"

Ellie caught up with him.

"That you're still involved with the boy's father?"

She stood in front of him.

"That's not true. Grant has been out of my life since six months after Kevin's birth."

"Where's your son, Ellie? Why haven't I met him? Or seen pictures of him?"

"Because he doesn't live with me."

Nathan's face twisted then seemed to register a new understanding.

"Oh. He lives with his father."

Ellie sighed and shook her head.

"No, we made an adoption plan. Kevin lives with his adoptive parents."

The blanched look Nathan gave her made her take a step back.

"What? You gave up your own child?!"

Creases dawned on her face as she struggled to understand his reaction.

"They're a wonderful family, Nathan."

"You gave away your child, your own child, Ellie."

His accusatory tone made the boil rising inside crest to a volcano. She tampered the explosion.

"I did what was best for him. His father and I did what was best for him."

"How could you give away your own son?"

"You weren't there. In fact, none of this has anything to do with you."

"I can't be involved with a woman who gives away her own child."

Nathan turned his back on her and began walking away again.

The volcano erupted and words spewed before Ellie could regain control.

"Who are you to judge me? You're an addict."

Nathan stopped. Then he turned, and when he looked at her, Ellie noticed his red face.

"I was that. I'm not now. You, however, are a mother, whether your son lives with you or not."

"That's right. I'm a mother. By giving birth."

"How can you deny your own flesh and blood, Ellie?"

She stared at him. Then she responded, "I don't deny ..."

"Well, you never told me," Nathan interrupted.

She stared at him and then took a deep breath. After exhaling, she said, "I would have, in time. In fact, I did try to tell you, but you wouldn't let me."

She seemed to catch him off-guard, so she chose to continue, in a more even voice, "Adoption is a gift, Nathan, for the parents and for the child, certainly my child. I didn't give Kevin away, I gave him a better life. He lives in a loving, stable home with great parents. I was a senior in college – I couldn't provide very well for him, and neither could his father. Grant and I tried to stay together, but ..." She shrugged. "Things didn't work out. We chose what we thought best for our son – another family, one with a mother and a father and stability. They could provide much better for him."

Nathan's stare created unease.

"I can't believe women give up their own children."

He turned again.

"You know, Nathan, it takes two to create a child."

That statement made him stop but he did not face her.

Ellie gritted her teeth and, in a seething tone, said, "Perhaps if men didn't turn their backs on us and if they cared a hoot about their child and the woman with whom they created that child, there wouldn't be as many abortions or adoptions. If men didn't leave us, more of us would feel loved and secure."

He turned around and stared at her. Ellie took another deep breath and let it out. Then she stated, "I made an open adoption plan, so I stay in touch with Kevin and his adoptive parents. We write, we talk, and sometimes we see each other. What does his birth father do? Nothing! No-thing!"

Nathan stared at her and said in a low, chastising tone, "If he had been my son, I wouldn't have given him to someone else."

"Kevin wasn't and isn't yours, so it's none of your business."

"You're right."

Nathan turned and began walking away again. Fury took root, and Ellie yelled, "Yep, just like Grant. Turn your back and leave me."

She noticed he stopped walking, but he didn't turn around to look at her.

"Just to be clear, Grant wanted nothing to do with the baby. He agreed to the adoption, and a few months later, he left me, turned his back on me just as you're doing. Men – you're all alike!"

She turned around and marched back to her cousin and mother.

THE LAST FEW SENTENCES Ellie spoke caused Nathan to hang his head. He turned to speak to her. He watched her walk away.

"What have I done?"

His muttered words and his overwhelmed brain made his heart drop to the pit of his gut. Yet, she had kept that important news from him, news of a child, with another man, a child she had given away. And he had learned the news not from Ellie, but from her mother.

Nathan shuffled to his truck parked nearby. He leaned against it feeling as weary as if he had worked on the greenhouse all day as he had done with Cal.

The greenhouse! Oh, man – I can't show up at the farm next week!

CHAPTER 27

E llie sat on the couch near the living room's picture window early the next morning, cup of steaming coffee in her hand. A light rain and the coolness of the dawn caused mist to rise from the nearby creek as heavy clouds hung over the mountains. Cecilia and Victor lay on the perches of the cat tree, the light gray tortoiseshell girl curled up in the circular bed at the top of the tree, while her larger, long-haired gray and white brother stood on the perch underneath, gazing out the window.

"Not a great morning for bird watching, is it, Victor?"

Ellie's whisper of his name caused the young cat to turn his golden eyes toward her.

"Not a great morning for much of anything."

Ellie felt a soft muzzle on her knee. She looked down into the amber eyes of Linda. The collie's long nose remained on Ellie's leg. Touched by this new show of affection, Ellie leaned down and patted the smooth fur of the dog's head. The tri-colored coat shone from the brushing bestowed yesterday, and Ellie stroked Linda's back. The dog leaned into her hand.

"Thank you for your trust, sweet girl," Ellie whispered. "Thank you for the comfort you're giving right now."

The collie's eyes remained on Ellie's face for a moment longer, then she turned and lay across Ellie's feet.

"I see you have friends already keeping you company. I was coming to do just that."

Maddy's statement caused Ellie to look up.

"It's nice to have them."

"Amen to that."

Maddy sat in the recliner.

"How are you doing?" she asked.

Ellie nodded toward the picture window.

"The weather says it all."

A moment of silence passed between them.

"I'm really sorry, Ellie. What your mother did... I don't think she intended .... What I mean is, she wasn't intentionally trying to hurt you or Nathan ..."

"I know. I should have told him sooner ..."

"You two haven't been together that long. You couldn't know ...."

"I tried to tell him after I learned about his opioid struggle. That would have been the better time, when he was sharing a private issue with me. I should have been bolder to tell him about my own past."

"Well, you said you tried and he wanted to wait and learn more of each other's pasts later – that's on him, not you."

"I should have tried harder."

Madison reached over and clasped Ellie's hand.

"No, cousin, you can't beat yourself up over this. Your mother spoke out of line. She shouldn't have assumed Nathan knew yet. Heck, you hadn't even told her about dating him. She's an intelligent woman – she just didn't show it yesterday."

Ellie sighed.

"One thing's for sure – I don't want her or my dad to set foot on this place again. I'm done with their drama and their lack of respect. Grandad left this farm to me, and it's up to me to make it successful. Despite all they've done to influence my choices, to derail my goals and dreams, to keep me from enjoying my life and finding my own success, I will succeed, and I will show them. I'll show them all, including Nathan!"

Maddy squeezed Ellie's hand.

"You don't need to show them, any of them. You need to do this for you. This is your home, your life, your dream. Your grandad knew you would succeed in keeping his legacy thriving. And you will succeed. I'll make sure of it."

"It's not up to you, Maddy."

"We're in this together."

Maddy took a deep breath, released it, and then squeezed Ellie's arm. She gazed out the window a moment and then looked at Ellie.

"I've been thinking about something for a few days," Maddy said. "I'm not going back to New Mexico. If you'll have me, I'd like to stay here. I want to set up art classes and teach as well as get back into painting. As I said yesterday, this place, the farm, the area, inspires me. I believe Merritt Valley is where I belong, and it's certainly where you belong."

"But Maddy – you have another year to finish your master's degree. You can't stop now."

"I don't intend to. I'll finish online and have the classes I teach and programs I create be my final project."

"Are you sure?"

Maddy smiled.

"Very."

Ellie clasped her cousin's hands.

"I'd love for you to stay!"

They hugged one another.

NATHAN SAT AT THE KITCHEN table, a pot of coffee in front of him and a cup of brew to his right. He gazed at the eastern sky through the patio doors. The rainfall began to subside, and the haze over the mountains started to lift, offering views of a crisp dawn in shades of rose and peach.

How could she not tell me about having a son? Why would she keep such a secret?

The questions still rolled in his mind, the same ones that kept him awake half the night.

Especially after I shared my opioid struggle with her just the night before.

He then remembered she had twice tried to tell him something, something she said she needed to share about her past. Realization struck.

Was that it? Was she trying to tell me about the boy and the adoption plan?

"Oh, man," Nathan whispered aloud.

His cell phone buzzed. He gazed at the caller ID: Jason. He let the call go to voicemail and took a sip of coffee from the nearby mug.

Another alert came from his phone, this time for an incoming text. He read a note from Ellie:

I find it interesting how I didn't let your news abt addiction &

recovery come between us, yet you don't give me the same courtesy.

"Well, you did throw it back in my face," he muttered.

And you turned your back on her.

The thought caused Nathan to sit up in his chair.

Did she turn her back on you when you told her about your addiction issue?

"I had to learn her secret from her mother," Nathan muttered aloud.

Looking at the text message again, he said, as if Ellie sat next to him, "You didn't hear my situation from someone else, you learned it from me."

Is that really fair? She did try to tell you and you put her off.

His brain waged war with his heart.

Another buzz. Another text. This one from Jason.

Hey, man. Checking in. Not seeing u at work is unsettling. U didn't drive over the mountain to Sweeney – Stevens said u took a sick day & that's not like you. Hope yr OK. Call me.

Nathan sighed and responded with a text back.

Sorry. Not feeling well. Will catch up w/ u later.

Nathan then stood and walked to the glass doors that looked upon the lake and the eastern sky. Soft hues of lavender, rose, and chiffon layered like a multi-flavored cake. Nature seemed sad this morning, just like he felt. As Nathan took another sip of coffee, his phone buzzed again.

"Ah, come on," he muttered.

He looked at another text from Jason.

Everyone makes mistakes & those of the past should stay in the past.

Nathan gaped at the words.

How does he know …?

Nathan sighed.

"The man's too smart for his own good," he mumbled.

Another blip and another message from Jason gave Nathan pause.

Love forgives. You do love her, don't you?

Nathan re-read the words and felt a nudging in his heart.

You didn't know her a decade ago. You know her now. She forgave you for your mess. So did Cal. He paid your mortgage for three months while you were in recovery.

His brain argued.

I never asked Cal to pay my mortgage.

His heart rejected that objection.

No. That's just the kind of man he was. And Ellie is like her grandparents. Are you more like your father or hers?

Nathan stared outside with sagging shoulders. After a moment, he dialed a familiar phone number. His father answered.

"Hey, Dad. How's things?"

He listened for a few minutes and then said, "Well, actually, not great. I learned last night some news that's shaken me. I could use some advice."

Nathan walked to the kitchen table and sat down again.

CHAPTER 28

That evening, Ellie and Maddy met the truck and trailer that ambled into the driveway. They heard the lambs baa, the donkeys bray, and the goats bleat from inside the long livestock trailer. They smiled at one another despite the commotion.

"They're finally here!"

Ellie's excitement appeared contagious, for Maddy commented, "Ooh, I can't wait to see them in person! I hope the noise means they're happy."

Ellie chuckled.

"Probably at least happy the truck and trailer aren't moving anymore."

Maddy laughed.

"I imagine so!"

"I'm glad Mr. Flannagan agreed to let the lambs be transported with the donkeys and goats," Ellie said. "That way, we get them all at the same time."

"And they're all here now," Maddy commented.

The truck driver leaped from the cab.

"Hi, ladies! Hope you're ready for these munchkins. Not easy getting them over those mountain passes on that two-lane highway."

"Yeah, those twists and turns can be tricky even without a livestock trailer," Ellie said. "We're glad you're here and that Angels Rescue hired you to bring them to us, and that you were able to bring the lambs from Mr. Flannagan's place. Each of these animals will have a wonderful home."

"All the stalls are ready," Maddy added. "We got them completed on Saturday."

The mention of that work-day and the troubles that came thereafter hit Ellie hard. Tears misted her eyes and she looked away. After blinking several times and composing herself, she looked at the driver and asked, "Do they have halters or do I need to gather some?"

"Halters already on. Connie said you can keep them. So did Mr. Flannagan."

Ellie nodded.

"That's very generous. Okay, let's get these critters settled in. Grace and Abby will be thrilled to have new neighbors and friends!"

She and Maddy began to follow the driver to the back of the trailer. Ellie paused when an alert came from her phone. She dug the cell out of the back pocket of her jeans to find a text from her mother.

"Not now," she mumbled and placed the cell phone back into the pocket.

Another beep. She ignored it and walked to the back of the trailer. Maddy looked at her.

"Everything okay?"

"Just mom. I'll read her texts later."

"You sure?"

"Oh, yeah. This day is too important to allow anything to spoil it!"

"Okay, ladies, meet your new charges," the driver announced.

He swung open the large, white metal door. Eight sets of eyes gazed at Ellie and Maddy through the green gate across the back of the trailer. Both women grinned.

"Oh, heavens! They're adorable!" Maddy said.

Ellie reached her hand through the gate and toward the nearest lamb, a black female with a white furry forehead. She scratched the little ears and then rubbed the lamb's nose. Ellie's eyes surveyed the group that included three lambs, three Pigmy goats, and two mini-donkeys. She turned her attention to the small goats, one gray and white, another black and gray, and the other caramel and white. Her heart softened from the blows of the past few days as she gazed at the animals.

She stroked the head of reddish-brown and white goat and murmured, "So sweet."

"I hope Connie told you that one's pregnant," the driver commented.

Ellie nodded.

"Twins, she said."

"Yep. Your herd will grow fast this year."

"We're fine with that," Maddy responded. "We're already planning products like goat milk soap and lotion."

"Lots of people like those things. Pretty big down in the Bitterroot."

"Well, let's get these animals to their new digs, shall we?"

Ellie's encouragement spurred Maddy to reach for the gate that covered the back end of the trailer. The driver blocked her path.

"Let me, miss. These guys are more used to me – best if I get them out and on the ground, one at a time."

Maddy nodded and stepped back, just as Ellie's phone buzzed again.

"Oh, good grief, she's persistent!"

Maddy looked at Ellie.

"Well, you haven't spoken to her since ...." She glanced at the driver. "Might want to see what she has to say."

Ellie studied her cousin then nodded and stepped to the side. Turning her back on Maddy and the driver, she checked the phone's screen. Seeing the call was from Nathan, Ellie hesitated. She took two more steps away and answered.

"I really can't talk now. The animals have arrived and I need to help get them ...."

"Ellie, just listen to me real quick. I'm sorry. I was wrong, and I was out of line. I really want to talk to you."

"I'm not sure I want to talk to you. Besides, I told you – this isn't a good time. Give me a few days. Maybe when you get back from the Sweeney River refuge ...."

"I asked Jason to take that assignment, starting tomorrow. I really want to work this out with you."

Ellie didn't respond right away.

"I don't know," she finally said.

"I'm sorry, Ellie, really I am. If you'll let me explain ..."

"I have animals to take care of."

She clicked off and turned around to see Maddy and the driver looking at her. She gave them a brief smile.

"Let's get these guys and girls moved, shall we?"

———— ❦ ————

NATHAN SAT ON THE GROUND of the local wildlife refuge, spotting scope nearby. He listened to the sounds of the land, the breeze rustling the greening grasses, the ripples of water on the nearby ponds, the warbling from songbirds, quacking of ducks, and honking of geese. He watched as two blue and gold dragonflies shimmered and danced near the cattails. A beaver splashed its tail near its dome-shaped lodge amid the larger pond, and a great blue heron waded in the marsh, likely searching for a meal. One sandhill crane poked its long beak into the sandy soil at the edge of the water, in search of bugs for a snack.

Nature's activity helped alleviate some of the heaviness stacked on Nathan's heart. He jotted observations in his small notebook and re-discovered some of the joy recently lost.

As the sun prepared to caress the nearby mountains for another evening, loud calls from sandhill cranes took root in the distance. Nathan turned his eyes toward the east. He watched two lanky birds with feet dangling approach the refuge's waters. He placed a pair of binoculars to his eyes and followed their movements. Closer and closer they came. He noted the bands on their legs, and he watched them land across the waterway from his study site. Nathan surveyed the parameters of the pond, and as his eyes captured the sight of two additional pairs of cranes, he smiled.

He made a decision. He pulled his cell phone from the carrier attached to his belt and texted Ellie.

More cranes at the refuge. I counted 5 pair this evening. Ur grandad would be really happy knowing the family farm is serving a bigger purpose – conservation.

After sending the message, Nathan returned to watching the birds. Additional ducks and geese also flew in. The rattle of antlers against a tree captured his attention. The binoculars focused on a large white-tailed buck cleaning velvet off its antlers against a cottonwood trunk. Nathan leaned down to view the scene with the spotting scope. His heart soared as he took in the sight of the grand buck, five spikes on the left antler and five on the right. Amid the trees, marsh meadows, and grasses wove small specks of color as wild iris, purple violets, and yellow bells painted the land. Spring at Merritt Valley Wildlife Refuge took deep root, creating a tranquility Nathan needed.

A blip from his phone diverted his attention. He unlatched the case and checked the text.

OK, I have to see that! R you at the refuge? If so, can I come by?

The peace from the landscape settled into his heart, and Nathan smiled. He texted back.

Yes & yes. I'll meet you at the gate.

CHAPTER 29

At the refuge twenty minutes later, Ellie sat on the ground near Nathan. She looked through the spotting scope, and her body relaxed when two pairs of sandhill cranes in different sections across from her observation point came into focus.

"Is that a nest near the banded pair?"

"Yeah. I believe they all have nests built now," Nathan replied.

Ellie looked at him.

"All five pair?"

He nodded and returned her gaze.

"The fifth must have constructed theirs as soon as they arrived. Each pair seems to have staked out their territory in different areas of the refuge. When I walked around the smaller pond, I noticed a nest on both sides of it as well as the ones over here."

"You're right – Grandad would have loved this!"

"You're still seeing the one crane come in to feed near the stream?"

She nodded.

"Not as often though."

"He's likely staying close to his mate more."

"I wondered that."

Ellie glanced at Nathan and then back toward the marsh. He reached out a hand, however, she kept hers on the spotting scope. Nathan let his hand drop.

"Ellie, I'm sorry," he whispered.

"You don't need to keep apologizing, Nathan."

"Yeah, yeah I do. I did the same thing with my sister."

"Your sister?"

She looked at him, and he nodded.

"She experienced an unplanned pregnancy five years ago. Stephanie is a bit younger than me. She was a sophomore in college. She made an adoption plan, a closed one, and none of us knows anything about the girl she had. I missed out on knowing my niece, and my parents missed the opportunity of spoiling a granddaughter. We were cheated."

"You resent her choice."

"I did, for a while. I thought I was over it, but when I learned about your son, well, I guess everything came rushing back. I felt like someone hit me on the back with a two-by-four."

"It's her life, Nathan, your sister's decision, at least hers and the baby's father, just as it was for Grant and me. We decided on open adoption because, although we weren't ready to raise our son, we wanted to be involved in his life."

"But what about your family? Your parents? Gr... Grant's parents? Didn't they deserve to get to know your baby?"

"Yes, that's what open adoption is about. My mother knew Kevin as a baby, but she's chosen to not be involved in his life, and my father, well, he's never wanted anything to do with my son."

"Oh, Ellie, I'm so sorry! I didn't realize ..."

She kept her eyes locked on his.

"No, you didn't because you wouldn't let me talk to you about it."

Nathan hung his head and slowly nodded.

"You're right," he said in a low voice. "I really am sorry."

Ellie placed a hand on his knee. He looked up at her.

"Do you want to know about Kevin?"

Nathan nodded. Ellie looked out toward the marsh, and, after a moment, she said in a soft voice, "Kevin is my son, the son I had with Grant while we were seniors in college. Obviously, the pregnancy was unplanned, and though I could have made a different decision, Grant and I agreed that would be selfish, and we made an open adoption plan with an adoption agency. I had our boy, and though I am his mother, the Mitchells are his family. They are wonderful people! They treat Kevin like he is their own birth child, but they respect me as his birth mother."

"So, the boy's father ... Grant ... he ... he's still involved in the boy's life? Do you two ever ... um, do you get together ... that is, see him at the same time?"

Ellie shook her head.

"Grant dropped out of Kevin's life about six years ago."

"He did? Why?"

Ellie shook her head.

"No one really knows. He just stopped corresponding and calling."

"Had to be hard on the boy."

"I'm sure it was. He's never really said anything to me, but his adoptive mother said he asked questions that first year and then hasn't mentioned anything about Grant again."

"And you – how often do you see him?"

"A few times a year. In fact, they're coming to the open house Memorial Day Saturday. Kevin wants to meet the animals."

"Oh."

A moment passed in silence. Ellie began to rise.

"Well, thank you for letting me see the cranes and all the spring sights that have popped up in the past few weeks. I'll keep good records of crane sightings at the farm."

Nathan caught her arm. She looked at him as he stood.

"Don't go yet, Ellie."

"I REALLY WANT US TO work out," Nathan heard himself saying. "There are some hurdles, but I'm hoping ... I hope you'll consider jumping over those with me."

He gazed into her eyes and studied her face.

"I was a jerk. I was a jerk to my little sister, too. And I regret my thoughts, my words, and my actions, to you and to her."

"Have you ... have you spoken with your sister since the adoption?"

"Yeah. Our relationship isn't as close as it once was, but we talk now and then."

"Maybe, as her big brother, she's wanting you to see beyond yourself. Unless you're a woman with an unplanned pregnancy, you have no idea the emotional rollercoaster that one goes on. And when the men, the important men, in your life, whether that's your partner, your dad, your brother, your grandfather, turn their backs on you, the loneliness is unfathomable."

"I never turned my back on my sister. I was there when she had the baby. So were our parents. The father – now he was a complete loser. When he found out Stephanie was pregnant, he not only dropped her like a hot potato, but he also left town. I guess he thought our dad would come after him or something."

"Or maybe he thought you would. Look, Nathan, you may have been there physically for your sister, but did you ever just let her talk? Talk about her fears, her concerns, her dreams, for herself or for her child? Did you just ever sit beside her and listen to her?"

Ellie's poignant questions dug up memories of times shared with Stephanie. With sadness, Nathan shook his head.

"That's probably what she needed," Ellie said. "That's what I needed. Fortunately, my grandparents did that for me, but, oh! how I longed for my father to do that, too. Even though we had a strained relationship and had for many years, I guess I thought when I was carrying his grandchild, he'd soften."

"You said they haven't met?"

Ellie shook her head.

"He refused. Mom stayed with me for a time even after the pregnancy. Dad never came once. Grammy and Grandad were also there when Kevin was born, and I came and lived with them for a time after the adoption. I also stayed with them when Grant left. Because of them I started working for the Park Service and went back for my master's degree. I honestly don't know where I'd be without their love and support. That's another reason the farm is extremely important to me – it became my refuge and my foundation for growing. And now, I'm helping it to grow. I want to, in honor of my grandparents."

"And you will. I believe in you, Ellie."

She tilted her head and studied his face.

"Why?"

"Because I see your strength. All you've done, including with your son, takes strength and perseverance. Your love for your family shines as well. All of that combines to make you the wonderful woman you are."

"You didn't think me so wonderful a few days ago."

Nathan clasped her hands in his, and his eyes searched her face.

"I was shocked by your news. You had every right to feel that way about what I told you as well. I really am sorry, Ellie, for how I reacted, for what I said, and for the fact your father wasn't there for you. I'm glad you had your grandparents, and I'm glad you have a relationship with Kevin and his family. I imagine he's quite a boy."

Ellie smiled.

"He is. He's bright, inquisitive, and fun. The Mitchells are raising him well."

"When they come visit, I hope I have the chance to meet them."

"You really want to?"

Nathan nodded.

"Yes, I really do."

He studied her face again.

"Will you forgive me and give us another chance?"

Her smile trembled.

"How could I not? You think I'm a wonderful woman."

Nathan returned her smile and then he leaned his head down and captured her lips with a gentle kiss. As he drew his mouth away, he leaned his forehead against hers.

"I love you, Ellie Davis."

The words came surprisingly easy because they came from his heart.

"I love you, too, Nathan Ford."

Hearing her softly-spoken words, gratitude welled up within Nathan. He held her in his arms and heard their hearts beat in time with one another.

With a slight smile, Nathan murmured, "So, if you want to add another special life to the Davis Family Farm, there's a wonderful dog named River in need of a loving home. What do you say – want to meet her?"

"I'd love to!"

CHAPTER 30

A few days later, Ellie stood in the larger corral next to the barn surrounded by twelve children. The dogs, Linda and River, sat in the middle of the circle, as if they, too, listened to her talk about them, the donkeys, lambs, goats, and horses.

"And that's why these different animals live here at Grandpa Cal's Animal Barn."

A boy about ten with hair the color of sunrise and freckles sprinkled across his nose raised his hand. Ellie acknowledged him with a smile and a nod.

"Yes?"

"Why are some people mean to animals?"

Ellie's smile faded.

"I don't know — maybe they didn't receive enough love or they're just selfish. Every person is different — some are more caring than others. But your being here, learning more about the animals and our responsibility to care for them shows me you're a kind person. And that's a good thing — you can share kindness to animals and people and teach them the importance of kindness and caring."

The boy nodded.

"I'm going to do that."

Ellie smiled at him.

"Good. I'm glad to hear that."

She looked around the group, smile still on her face.

"Now, who wants to meet the animals?"

A chorus of cheers and *"Yeahs!"* rose up. Ellie looked at Maddy, who waited by the gate. The large enclosure contained the lambs, two goats, both mini-donkeys, and Grace.

"Miss Maddy will introduce you to them," Ellie told the children.

She noticed Nathan approaching from the wine-tasting tent set up near the vineyard gazebo. She looked at the children again.

"I'll join you all in a moment. Remember the rules — approach the animals quietly and pet them gently."

The youngsters didn't say a word as they walked toward Maddy. With a smile, Ellie's cousin opened the gate and then said, "Okay, let's go and make some animal friends, but please do so quietly, like Miss Ellie said. We don't want to scare them."

Ellie and Nathan met part-way between the edge of the vineyard and the barn.

"How's the wine tasting going?"

"Good, great in fact. Everyone loves your grandfather's wine. But you need to know — your parents are here."

Ellie attempted to keep her composure.

"Oh, man – not what I need, today of all days! I didn't think mom would remember the open house date."

"Well, you've been getting a lot of publicity. Likely they saw something."

She nodded.

"The bad part about P.R."

Nathan took her hands in his, looked into her olive eyes, and said, "Well, the day is a success. They've got to see how great your whole idea is."

Ellie gave him a wobbly smile.

"Thanks in large part to you."

He smiled.

"We make a good team. Your vision, your business plan, Maddy's creative design and beautiful paintings, me the project executioner and media hounder– we work well together."

He leaned over and kissed her cheek. Afterward, he asked, "Want me to go with you?"

Ellie shook her head.

"We have twelve kids in the pen, and Maddy's by herself. Would you help her, please? I'll be all right with my parents. If I have to, I'll ask them to leave – I've done it before."

"I hope you don't have to."

She nodded.

"Me too."

"Jason's up there if you need anything. He'll stand alongside you."

"He's become a good friend."

Nathan gave her a slight smile.

"He's a good guy. I'm glad Maddy's been able to look beyond his flaws, and that he's taking strides to change."

"We all need a little help in certain areas of our lives. Change and forgiveness are big steps."

She kissed his cheek and then whispered, "I'm glad we've taken those steps ... together."

"Me, too."

Ellie took a deep breath and then released it.

"Wish me luck."

"You've got this. I believe in you, Ellie."

She smiled.

"I know, and I'm grateful."

Catching sight of her parents standing near the tent, she raised her chin as she strode confidently toward them.

NATHAN WATCHED ELLIE walk toward the wine-tasting area. He noticed the determination in her stride, and he grinned.

Go get 'em, girl!

He felt love for her and pride for her accomplishments grow like summer wildflowers, bright and tall, securely rooted. He knew he had nearly blown his chance with her in his selfishness. He had acted like her father instead of his own. His dad had always shown support and care for him, even during his opioid downfall, and he had served as his strongest cheerleader during recovery. Nathan regretted that reaction to the news of Kevin's existence, and he felt thankful for the millionth time that month for the restoration of his relationship with Ellie.

Nathan paused, pulled his cell phone out of his pants pocket, and hit speed dial. The man on the other end answered, and Nathan smiled.

"Hey, Dad. Just wanted to call and say hi, see how you're doing. Summer's finally come to western Montana."

He paused as he listened to his father, then, a few moments later, responded, "Yeah, the Open House at Ellie's farm is underway. It's been a great turnout so far."

He listened for a few more minutes.

"Well, wish I was there to go with you. You and mom need to come out this fall so I can take you fishing. And you can meet Ellie."

Another few moments.

"Yeah, Dad, thanks. We're doing great. I appreciate that kick in the butt you gave me. All I could focus on was Stephanie's decision and what we've missed as a family."

He listened again then responded, "Kevin seems like a good kid. And they do have a good relationship. I'm glad I was able to meet him."

Nathan glanced up and saw Maddy waving at him.

"Hey, Dad, I need to go – Maddy needs my help with the group of kids she's trying to corral."

Another pause and then a chuckle.

"Sure, I like that idea. We'll Facetime tomorrow evening, you, me, mom, and Ellie. Talk with you then. And Dad – thanks for everything. I've never really said it before, but I really appreciate all the times you were there for me, encouraging me, helping me. You and Mom – well, just know I'm really grateful to you both and thankful we're family."

Another pause.

"Love you, too, Dad. Talk with you tomorrow."

He hung up and walked toward the corral. As he did, his eyes darted around the property. People milled about, some adults sipping wine while others, with kids, stopped near the corrals and barn to view the lambs, goats, and donkeys. The foal, born to Abby three days ago, frolicked beside her mother in pasture behind the barn, the youngster's silver-gray coat sparkling in the sunlight.

Nathan recalled his conversation with Ellie the night the small horse was born after the veterinarian and Mr. Flannagan had departed.

"Your menagerie continues to grow," he said to Ellie.

"Yes. The foal and all the others bring joy to me and Maddy," she had replied. "They'll bring joy to our visitors as well. I think the open house is going to be successful, and as Madison and I add new products and programs to the farm's offerings, I can foresee the expansion of the Davis Family Farm."

"I have no doubt."

His arms encircled her.

"I want to see you succeed, Ellie, and I'm positive you will. I believe in your vision and goals. Cal and Marie would be very proud of you, and I'm sure they're smiling on you right now."

Her tight hug and gentle kiss caused him to shiver at the memory. And, to think, he had nearly messed everything up. He recalled the text Jason had sent several days ago: **Love forgives.**

Ellie certainly must love him, for she had forgiven him. He knew he certainly loved her.

Nathan glanced around again and saw Ellie standing near the wine-tasting tent, her parents nearby. No animation, nor flaying arms, no raised voices.

So far, so good.

He then looked toward the corrals again and caught Maddy's eye. Her flushed face displayed overwhelm, and she frantically beckoned him to assist with the group of children, a few of whom were chasing chickens. About that time, the two adopted farm dogs dashed to his side, barking. He smiled at the friendship Linda and River had quickly developed.

"Okay, okay, I'm getting the message," he told the dogs. "Let's go!"

Nathan jogged alongside the collie and the lab toward the corral.

CHAPTER 31

Ellie stood near the gazebo at edge of the vineyard. Maddy's three paintings, two of the farm and one of the wildlife refuge, hung amid the strings of white lights in the enclosure. Her heart filled with joy at her cousin's creativity and the joy and attention given to them by those attending the open house. However, seeing her parents, delight was replaced with wariness.

Each dressed in business casual attire, her father in khaki pants with a blue, print long-sleeved shirt, and her mother wearing pastel green linen pants with a sea-green and cream short-sleeved top; a cream knit coverlet added to the ensemble. Each held a wine glass half-filled with Grandad's cabernet.

Ellie nodded at them.

"Mom. Dad. I wasn't expecting you."

Her parents glanced at one another.

"Uh, er, it was your mother's suggestion."

Ellie looked at her father.

"Honestly, I'm most surprised you showed up, Dad. I'm asking both of you to please not cause a scene. This has been a good day so far, and I don't need any family drama."

"Eleanor," her mother began.

"I mean it, Mother. You nearly destroyed a relationship I wanted to see grow. Thankfully, Nathan and I have worked things out."

"I'd say it was your actions, or should I say, inactions, that caused the problems."

Ellie looked at her father again and gave him a frown.

"Your tart and snide comments aren't welcome here, Dad, and frankly, neither are you. This is my property, and if you're going to be rude and disrespectful to me, you can leave."

Ellie turned on her heel and began to walk back toward the corral. Her mother's hand upon her arm, hesitant yet convincing, gave her pause.

"Eleanor, I'm sorry. We are sorry. That's why we came. We want you to know we love you and ... and we're proud of you."

Ellie slowly turned to face her parents.

"What?"

She glanced from one to the other. A brief time of silence passed between them.

"I think you heard your mother," her father finally said.

Ellie stared at him and then shook her head.

"I should have known better. You really don't want to apologize, do you, Dad? You're just here to see if I continue to disappoint you."

"No, Eleanor, that's not true. It's not you. It's ... it's this place."

Bruce Davis took a deep breath and looked around the property.

"For years, I hated this farm. I watched my own father work sunrise to after sunset, struggling year after year after year. This property nearly killed him many times – almost killed me a few times too – and I hated it."

He looked at Ellie.

"You saw the farm during the better years, once pastures, orchards, and gardens were in place. The animals my dad raised were able to grow fat off those grasses, and the vegetables, fruit, and herbs my parents grew and sold became sustenance for the residents and then the visitors. All you know is the good, not the bad and the ugly."

"I've seen plenty of ugly, Dad – the way you treated Grammy and Grandad, your own parents. And then how you treated me, your daughter. No, Dad, the bad and the ugly came from you, not from the farm."

She turned to walk away but decided to face her parents again with the rest of what she wanted to say.

"I hope you both enjoy your visit to the Davis Family Farm, soon to become Merritt Valley Farm and Animal Sanctuary. New owner, new business, new name, new mission. And it's going to be a great success because of its legacy and vision. What Grammy and Grandad started and foresaw I intend to see to fruition and grow to a higher level with thanks to friends and community, but with no thanks to you. Enjoy yourselves, as much as you can at this place you despise, but don't feel the need to stay."

Ellie turned away again but the next words from her father gave her pause.

"I'm sorry, Eleanor."

She remained with her back turned to her parents.

"I'm sorry that I've hurt you and that I've not been supportive."

Ellie turned slowly and looked at him.

"Those are words, Dad, and at this point, they don't mean anything."

"I haven't been a very good father. I let certain ... expectations and then disappointments prevent me from being better."

"So, you were, are, disappointed in me." She shook her head and then said, "You could have chosen to accept me for who I am. You could have chosen to forgive me of my mistakes, but no – you lorded them over me."

She shook her head again and added, "Oh, what's the point? Enjoy the wine, made by Grandad, by the way. Mingle a bit if you want, then just leave. And please – don't tell people we're related and how disappointed you are in me."

She turned on her heel.

"Mama Ellie!"

Kevin's excited voice caused her to stop. Ellie composed herself and then, with a smile, she turned around to see the eight-year-old rushing toward her. Her smile broadened as he flung his arms around her waist.

"I got to ride Grace again!"

She lowered herself to Kevin's height and hugged him.

"That's wonderful, Kevin! Grace is a nice horse, isn't she?"

"The best!"

He stepped away to look into her face. Over the boy's shoulder, Ellie saw Kevin's adoptive parents striding toward them, smiles on their faces.

"I can see why she was Grandpa Cal's favorite. I love her!"

Ellie chuckled and stood. She noticed Kevin looking at her parents and that they returned the little boy's gaze. Kevin stuck out his hand to Ellie's father.

"I'm Kevin Mitchell."

Ellie's parents looked at her. She took the lead. Placing her hands on the boy's shoulders, she said, "Kevin, I'd like you to meet ... friends of Grandpa Cal's. This is Mr. Bruce and Miss Julie."

The boy's blue eyes, so much like Grant's, she recalled, widened.

"You knew my Grandpa Cal? Well, I guess he was really my great-grandpa, Mama Ellie's real grandpa, but I kind of feel like he was my grandpa, too. I met him when I was really little, like five or six, but only for a short time. Mama Ellie told me last year he died."

Ellie looked at Kevin's adoptive parents.

"Jordan and Whitney Mitchell, this is, uh, Bruce and Julie. Bruce, uh, used to live around here."

As the adults shook hands and exchanged greetings, Kevin looked again at Ellie's father with wide eyes.

"You lived here? So, you did know Grandpa Cal!"

"Yes, yes, I knew him. I, uh, I grew up in the valley," Ellie's father responded.

"Cool! You were lucky! This is a really neat place, and my Mama Ellie here is going to make it ever neater!"

Bruce smiled, a sight Ellie hardly fathomed. Her knees weakened and she held on to Kevin's shoulders, giving them a squeeze. Her son looked up at her.

"Are you okay, Mama Ellie?"

She gave him a brief smile and responded, "Yes, Kevin. I'm glad you and your mom and dad are enjoying yourselves."

"Miss Maddy said Abby's foal was born. Can I see it?"

"In a little bit. That's a special treat only for you and your parents."

A large smile came to the boy's face.

"Cool!"

Ellie's dad bent down toward the boy.

"What's your favorite part about the farm, Kevin?"

"The animals! I really like Grace, the horse, and Mama Ellie's two dogs. Grandpa Cal had a dog like Linda once – I met that dog when I little, too."

"I knew that dog, too. Her name was Angel."

"You were lucky to live here," Kevin repeated.

"Yes, yes, I guess you're right."

Bruce stood to his six-foot height. Ellie glanced at him and then caught her mother's eye. Tears glistened in the corners. Julie turned her face away from the group, and Ellie hugged her son's shoulders.

"Have you seen all the animals Mama Ellie has?" Kevin asked as he looked at the grandfather he didn't know.

Bruce shook his head and replied, "No, not yet."

"The donkeys are really cute! So are the goats! There's a real tiny one in the corral. And two little sheep."

"What are they called, do you remember, Kevin?" Jordan asked.

"Lambs, that's what Miss Maddy said."

"Good memory, son," Whitney praised him. "You were listening – good job!"

Kevin grinned at his adoptive parents and then turned to Bruce once again.

He held out his small hand toward Ellie's father.

"Come on, I can show you all the animals."

Ellie's heart swelled to see the innocence and acceptance Kevin had toward her parents, especially with the grandfather he didn't know. Keeping her tears at bay, she took her son's hand and crouched down again to look into his sparkling eyes.

"Tell you what, Kevin. Would you and your mom and dad go back to the barn and tell Mr. Nathan and Miss Maddy that I'll be down in just a few minutes? Wait for us, and you can ride Grace again. When I get down there, Mr. Nathan and I will take you and your parents to see Abby's baby."

The boy's blue eyes widened and he exclaimed, "Cool!"

Ellie looked at Jordan and Whitney.

"If that's okay with your parents."

Whitney smiled.

"I think that's a fine idea."

"Come on, Kev," Jordan said, reaching out his hand to the boy. "Let's see if those donkeys will let us pet them again and if anyone is riding Grace. If not, you can get up on her and ride while we wait for Mama Ellie."

Kevin took his father's hand, and Ellie stood.

"Okay, Dad. I like Grace and the donkeys. And the goats, too."

"I'll introduce you to my chickens and cats later," Ellie said.

Kevin looked at her.

"You have chickens? And cats?"

Ellie smiled.

"Six chickens and two cats. I'll send some eggs home with you and your parents, and you can eat them for breakfast."

"Cool! Mom makes yummy cheese omelets."

Looking at Whitney, Ellie said, "I bet she does."

Kevin's adoptive parents smiled, and then each took hold of one of the boy's hands. As they walked back toward the barn, the eight-year-old skipped between them.

NATHAN STOOD AT THE corral watching the Davis family and Kevin and his adoptive parents. He longed to know what words were being exchanged. He had witnessed some animation earlier, in between giving children rides on Grace and wrangling others from the lambs and chickens. Now the area was quieter. Nathan took a few steps from the enclosure. He felt a tender hand upon his arm. He turned to look at Madison.

"Let them be for a bit. There's a lot of family history and drama with them and hopefully, they are working all that out."

"Ellie's told me some of the issues, particularly with her dad," Nathan responded. "I don't want to see her hurt again."

"Neither do I, but we need to give them space and give her opportunity to stand up for herself. Besides, I see Kevin and his parents headed back here. This will give you a chance to know the boy better, something you should do if you plan to be part of Ellie's life."

Nathan stared into her eyes. Then, he nodded.

"I do intend to be a big part of her life. Yeah, you're right."

Maddy smiled and then whispered, "I found one of Cal's old cowboy hats in the barn the other day when we worked in there. I hung it on a hook. I think Kevin might like it."

Nathan followed her into the large, wooden building. Maddy pointed out the straw hat, crinkled from use and weather. A turquoise and white band encircled the topper, and a turkey feather was tucked on the side. Nathan collected the piece and returned outside. When Kevin and his parents arrived, Nathan asked, "Are you back for another ride on Grace?"

"Yes, sir!"

Nathan bent down and presented the hat to Kevin.

"Well, every cowboy needs a good hat, and I think Grandpa Cal would like you to have one of his."

The boy's blue eyes widened.

"This belonged to Grandpa Cal?"

Nathan smiled.

"Sure did, and now it's yours whenever you visit."

"Cool!"

Nathan glanced at Maddy, who smiled. Then, he stood.

"I think Grace is ready for you," he said to Kevin.

As Jordan and Kevin followed Maddy into the corral, Kevin turned to do the same. Whitney's hand on his arm stopped him, and he looked at her.

"I'm so glad you and Ellie found each other," the woman whispered. "You're really great together. You know, she gave Jordan and I a great gift in that little boy, and we will always be grateful. Grant may be out of her life and out of Kevin's life, but I'm glad you're in hers ... and now in our lives and the life of our son. I'm thankful for that."

She gave him a brief smile and a quick nod then followed Madison and her family into the corral. Nathan glanced at them and then up the hill toward Ellie and her parents. He saw movement along the hillside above the stream at the back of the house. His eyes widened at what he saw.

CHAPTER 32

"Such a handsome boy!"

Ellie looked at her mother.

"Yes, he is. And smart."

"He looks like you, Ellie."

She looked at her father. She noticed water misted his eyes.

"He loves animals, just like you," Bruce said.

Tears threatened to leak from her eyes.

"He's certainly a part of me and a part of Grant. And a big part of Grandad. I want Kevin to know this part of his heritage."

"He certainly seems to be taking to it, especially with the changes you've made," her father said in a hushed tone.

Then he broke.

"Oh, daughter, I'm so sorry! So sorry for hurting you and failing to try to understand."

Ellie bit her lip and attempted to remain stoic. However, her mother's words cracked more armor.

"I'm sorry, too, Ellie. I'm sorry I spoke out about something that was not my place to talk about. I do hope you and Nathan can put aside your parents' lack of grace and that you both will eventually forgive us. You know I'd never intentionally hurt you – Ellie, you're my only daughter, and I dearly, dearly love you!"

Tears spilled from Ellie's eyes. She glanced away and then looked at them.

"All I ever wanted was your support, your respect, your understanding."

She searched her parents' faces.

"And to know that you love me in spite of our differences and despite my failures."

"We do, dear," her mother replied, tears trailing on her cheeks.

"I'm the failure," Bruce stated, water saturating his eyes. "Seeing Kevin, listening to him, I know that now. I probably always knew it but was too stubborn and prideful to admit it."

Julie wiped her eyes and placed a hand on Bruce's arm. She looked at Ellie and whispered, "We both failed you, in so many ways."

She glanced at her husband and then returned her eyes to Ellie.

"All of us experience failure at some point, whether in our jobs, as parents, as human beings – it's a part of life. But, as your father said, pride and stubbornness sometimes keep us from admitting those mistakes. I hope you will forgive me, forgive both of us."

Ellie gave her mother a wobbly smile.

"Thank you, Mom. I do appreciate you being there when I needed you – when Kevin was born, when Grant left, when I started my career, and when I decided to pursue my master's degree. And forgive me that I forgot that and asked you to leave the farm a few weeks ago."

Julie released her husband's arm and enveloped Ellis in an embrace. Afterward she looked at her father.

"I wasn't there for you like your mother," Bruce stated. "I know I'm asking a lot, but I do ask for your forgiveness. I wasn't a good father. But I want to be. Will you let me be part of your life or is it too late?"

She gave him a small smile.

"You know, Dad, this place belonged to your parents. If you really want, we can start over. The farm is your legacy and heritage as much as it is mine. Stay a few days. Spend time getting to know the place where you grew up."

Bruce reached out his hand. Ellie clasped both of hers in his, and then Bruce laid his other hand atop their entwined fingers. His walnut-colored eyes looked into her olive ones.

"And getting to know my daughter again?"

Ellie smiled.

"I'd like that. Who knows? You might find you don't hate the farm anymore."

He smiled.

"I've already come to love it." He looked around. "You're doing amazing things here, Eleanor. Family-oriented activities, healthy food, delicious wine."

"And don't forget animal rescue," Julie chimed in.

Bruce's smile enlarged.

"Something my mother had wanted to do."

Ellie's gray-green eyes widened.

"Really? I never knew that."

Her father chuckled.

"Oh, the stories I could share!"

Ellie's smile trembled.

"I hope you will."

Her father's gray eyes locked with her olive ones.

"I shall."

He opened his arms and she stepped into his embrace. Julie wrapped her arms around both of them, and the family hugged one another.

As Ellie stepped from her parents' embrace, she saw a pair of sandhill cranes strolling near the stream behind the farmhouse. Between the adult birds hopped a yellow chick. Ellie's breath caught.

"Mom, Dad – look!" she whispered.

They turned, and she pointed.

"A family of sandhill cranes! Right here on the property!"

Her low voice contained excitement.

"My!" Bruce said as he stared at the birds. "I haven't seen cranes here since I was a boy!"

"What a sight!" Julie whispered.

Another large smile came to Ellie's face, and she placed her arms around her parents' shoulders.

"They're welcoming you back, Dad. It's like Grammy, Grandad, and you – two parents and a youngster."

Her father chuckled, a sound she rarely heard during the past decade.

"You may be right, Ellie, you just may be right."

NATHAN JOGGED TO THE Davis family, glancing now and then at the sandhill crane family. Upon reaching Ellie's side, he whispered, "Did you see?"

Her smile provided affirmation before her words.

"Yes. Amazing isn't it?"

"We definitely need to document this!"

Bruce stepped forward, his hand held out to Nathan. The two men looked at each other.

"Thank you for all you did for my father, Nathan, and for what you're doing for my daughter. I'm glad you're in her life."

Nathan accepted the outstretched hand and clasped it.

"My honor and pleasure, sir. Ellie is quite the woman."

He smiled at the auburn-haired woman. She returned his gaze and smile.

"Would you like a tour of the vineyard?" Nathan asked Bruce and Julie. "Cal planted a wonderful batch of grapes, and they're growing gangbusters already this spring."

"I'd like that, and if the two of you are interested, I have a few ideas for marketing the wine in Missoula."

"We'd love to hear your ideas, Dad," Ellie said. "How about dinner tonight? We're all going to need to put our feet up this evening."

"I think that sounds lovely, don't you, Bruce?"

Nathan noticed Julie look at her husband with shining eyes. He glanced at Ellie, and when their eyes met, he noticed a similar glow of love.

"Yes, yes, it does. Is the Shoreliner still open?"

Bruce's question caused Ellie and Nathan to smile at each other and then at her parents.

"Yes, sir, it certainly is."

Bruce placed his arm around Julie's waist, and, looking at her, said, "I proposed to Julie there, along the water's edge, and then we had dinner to celebrate our engagement."

"I remember Grammy sharing that story with me," Ellie said. "Didn't Grandad propose to her there as well?"

Bruce grinned. "Sure did. In that way, I followed in my father's footsteps."

Nathan filed the news in his brain ... and his heart.

EPILOGUE

Nathan and Ellie strolled near the corrals and barn as twilight took root two weeks later. The dogs, Linda and River, padded beside them.

"Another beautiful Merritt Valley night," Nathan commented, Ellie's hand warmly tucked into his.

"I don't know if I've ever experienced a more beautiful sky than here," she replied.

"Oh, I think every sky unobstructed by buildings possesses beauty. I'm sure you experienced many gorgeous mornings and evenings at Saguaro."

"I did. I think these are extra glorious to me, though, because of the tranquility I feel here, the connection to my family."

"Speaking of family, when your parents come up tomorrow and my parents arrive for their planned visit, where shall we go to dinner? You said this morning you'd give me an answer."

"Yes, yes, I did say that. What do you think of a dinner cruise on the lake?"

He looked at her.

"We should have made reservations several days ago. I'm sure they're booked up."

"As of noon, they still had ten seats available. It's mid-week, and tourist season is just starting, so they had availability. I reserved eight, just in case you thought it a good idea, too. We have until ten tomorrow morning to cancel."

"Oh, I think it's a splendid idea! I know my parents will love it. What about yours?"

"I think the cruise will help Dad reconnect even more to the area. I remember Mom telling me years ago that was one activity they enjoyed together here in the valley."

"Great! Then, that's what we'll do. Wait – you said you reserved eight seats. Don't we need just seven? I'm assuming you counted Maddy."

Ellie smiled. She stopped walking and looked at Nathan.

"I thought you might want to invite Jason."

Nathan grinned.

"Ah, scheming, are you?"

Ellie's smile widened.

"I think they just got off on the wrong foot. A second chance doesn't hurt. Besides, they seemed to enjoy the outing to Sweeney River Refuge we took last weekend"

"Nope, second chances certainly don't hurt. And you're right – they do seem to have mended fences."

"Beautiful scenery and amazing wildlife sightings can have that affect."

"Seeing the elk cows with their calves did seem to have a positive influence on the entire day."

"Not to mention the trumpeter swans with their cygnets."

"And the moose cow and calf."

"And the wildflowers."

"And now another beautiful painting from your cousin with hang in your newly-established gallery."

"I'm so glad Maddy's staying. Finishing her master's online, teaching classes in the valley this fall, planning an art exhibit, and helping me with the orchard will keep her very busy, and very happy, I'm sure."

Nathan drew Ellie into his arms.

"You make me very happy, you know that?"

She smiled and wrapped her arms around his neck.

"I'm happy to know that ... because you make me very happy, too."

Their lips met in a sweet, soft kiss.

Drawing back, Nathan whispered, "I'm glad you've given me a second chance, that you're giving us a second chance."

"Forgiveness is the heart of every relationship," Ellie said with a slight smile.

He tightened his grip.

"That it is."

He then clasped her hand into his again and they continued their stroll to the corrals. Inside each enclosure, the lambs, goats, mini-donkeys, horses, and chickens ate their evening meals. Nathan paused to watch.

"The animals seem to be thriving."

"I think Grandpa Cal's Animal Barn is going to be a hit with families."

"Well, if the open house gives any indication, the program certainly will be a hit. Kevin will be your word-of-mouth advertising."

Ellie smiled.

"He's an amazing little boy."

Nathan looked at her again.

"His mom's amazing, too."

Ellie studied his face and gave him a small smile.

"You're pretty great yourself."

Nathan brought their clasped hands to his mouth, and, while looking into her eyes, tenderly kissed the knuckles.

The distinct call of sandhill cranes caused Ellie and Nathan to look up. As shades of apricot, periwinkle, and rose touched the evening sky, two of the large birds flew overhead, traveling from the farm toward the refuge.

"Whenever I see sandhill cranes, I think of my grandparents," Ellie said in a soft voice. "I know they mate for life, just like swans. I can't help but think of them when I see either type of bird."

"Love in flight," Nathan said.

They looked at each other and smiled then returned their gaze to the twilight sky. Nathan's eyes caught a glimmer of light.

"Uh," he said. "Our banded pair!"

"How do you know they're banded?"

Nathan pointed at the birds' outstretched legs.

"See that glint of silver?"

Ellie stared and in a moment she noticed a glimmer from one of the crane's legs.

With excitement, she said, "Oh, yes, I do see. So beautiful!"

When Nathan didn't respond, Ellie looked at him and found a small smile on his face.

Looking into her eyes, he whispered, "Certainly is. Most definitely beautiful."

Their lips found one another and danced together in a cadence of admiration, gratitude, love and passion.

About Gayle M. Irwin

Gayle M. Irwin is an award-winning Wyoming author and freelance writer who has been recognized by Wyoming Writers, Inc. and the Wyoming Press Association for several of her works. She is a contributing writer in eight *Chicken Soup for the Soul* books, including the January 2023 release "Lessons Learned From My Dog." Gayle is the author of many inspirational pet books for children and adults, including *A Dog Named Mary Visits Yellowstone National Park*, *Sage Finds Friends*, and *Walking in Trust: Lessons Learned With My Blind Dog*. She also writes a sweet, contemporary romance series set in the Yellowstone National Park area, where she lived for nearly 12 years. Gayle considers herself a pet rescue advocate and assists various rescue organizations in different ways, such as serving as a volunteer transporter and by donating a percentage of book sales to such groups. Learn more on her website: gaylemirwin.com

Also by GAYLE M. IRWIN

Pet Rescue Romance
Rescue Road
My Montana Love
Finding Love at Compassion Ranch
Grams' Legacy
Rhiann's Rescue - Pet Rescue Romance Series Prequel
Paws-ing for Love: A Pet Rescue Christmas Story

Standalone
Love Takes Flight

Watch for more at https://gaylemirwinauthor.com/.